W9-BVF-828

"Of course it's my business, Griffin,"

his mother dismissed scathingly. "You're my son."

"But being your son does not give you the right—especially at thirty-four years of age!—to choose my friends for me! Or the woman I marry," he added forcefully.

"But—"

"You seem determined that I marry someone, Mother, so—" he moved slightly so that he could place his arm around Dora's shoulders "—I would like you to meet your future daughter-in-law, Isadora Baxter!"

Dora drew in a sharp breath, not sure who was the more shocked by his triumphant announcement—his mother or herself!

CAROLE MORTIMER says, "I was born in England, the youngest of three children—I have two older brothers. I started writing in 1978, and have now written over one hundred books for Harlequin®.

"I have four sons—Matthew, Joshua, Timothy and Peter—and a bearded collie called Merlyn. I'm married to Peter senior, we're best friends as well as lovers, which is probably the best recipe for a successful relationship. We live on the Isle of Man."

Books by Carole Mortimer

HARLEQUIN PRESENTS®

Carole Mortimer

THEIR ENGAGEMENT IS ANNOUNCED

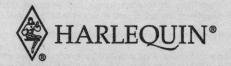

TORONTO • NEW YORK • LONDON
AMSTERDAM • PARIS • SYDNEY • HAMBURG
STOCKHOLM • ATHENS • TOKYO • MILAN • MADRID
PRAGUE • WARSAW • BUDAPEST • AUCKLAND

Peter,
As Always.

ISBN 0-373-12098-2

THEIR ENGAGEMENT IS ANNOUNCED

First North American Publication 2000.

Copyright © 2000 by Carole Mortimer.

This edition published by arrangement with Harlequin Books S.A.

Visit us at www.romance.net

Printed in U.S.A.

CHAPTER ONE

THE bell over the shop doorway rang as cheerfully as usual to announce the arrival of a customer. Its innocent sound did nothing to alert her to the fact that this customer was going to be any different from any other she'd had in today, that Griffin Sinclair was about to burst into her life—again!

'Izzy? Izzy! I just called in to— Good God, woman, what the hell have you done to yourself? Your erstwhile fiancé, my dear brother Charles, has been dead almost a year now. Did no one tell you that the deceased's nearest and dearest no longer have to wear black for a whole year, let alone throw themselves on the funeral pyre with them?'

She had felt her blood turn to ice at the first sound of that mocking voice, but the words that followed shocked her so much that she couldn't even speak!

She had always found this man's outspokenness, his whole overpowering personality uncomfortable to be around. And despite the fact that she hadn't seen him since Charles's funeral ten months ago—it was exactly ten months ago—today was no exception!

'Izzy, are you ill?' He frowned across at her where she sat behind the desk that also housed the till, his brows narrowed over emerald-green eyes. 'Izzy?' he prompted again, impatient now at her lack of response.

'Dora.' She finally spoke softly.

'What?' Griffin scowled his irritated impatience.

'My name is Dora,' She told him more firmly, recovering slightly from the shock of seeing him again. 'And would you either come in or go out of that doorway? You're letting in a draught!'

He came fully into the shop, the bell over the door ringing again as he closed it behind him. 'You know, I've never liked the name Dora.' He arrogantly dismissed her first statement, grinning his satisfaction now that he had at least got some sort of response from her.

He looked, Dora decided, completely incongruous in the intimate confines of this speciality bookshop. His denims were as old and faded as the brown boots he wore, a black tee-shirt was tucked in at his flat waist, and a brown leather jacket seemed to have been thrown on carelessly over this. But for all his seeming indifference to the clothes he wore, his physique was powerful with vitality, like a lion about to pounce. Dora just wished she didn't feel quite so much like the prey he intended pouncing upon!

He really was the most unorthodox man she had ever seen, Dora decided. His hair was even longer than when she had last seen him, golden waves of it reaching to his shoulders now, looking as if the most he did with it was run his fingers through it in the mornings just to push it back off his face. And the length of that unruly hair was totally off-set by the rugged strength of his face, which looked as if it had been hewn from stone: a square chin, full lips, straight, arrogant nose, and those deep green eyes. At the moment he was still grinning at her, those green eyes laughing at her, forcing lines to appear beside his eyes and mouth.

In fact, Griffin Sinclair was so altogether male that he set Dora's teeth on edge! A fact that had always made it difficult for her to believe he really was Charles's younger brother.

'I don't believe it's actually significant whether or not you actually like my name, Griffin—'

'Oh, I love your name—Izzy,' He drawled pointedly. 'And I quite like Isadora. It's only Dora that I can't stand.' He grimaced with feeling. 'It makes you sound like a Dickensian heroine!'

She raised her auburn brows. 'You meant you dislike the *name* Dora, of course,' she taunted dryly—no one ever called her Isadora.

Griffin strolled further into the shop, his derisive expression showing exactly what he thought of the shelves and shelves of non-fiction and classical books that surrounded the two of them.

'Of course,' he agreed softly, standing only feet away from her now. 'Dora sounds like an old maid, and old-fashioned to boot.' Once again his critical gaze swept over her sombre clothing.

And Dora knew exactly what he would see, too. The black calf-length skirt and black jumper were completely unflattering to either her figure or the natural paleness of her complexion. Only the vibrant red of her own shoulder-length hair gave her any colour at all, and that was secured at her nape with a black ribbon.

'Isadora is coolly elegant,' Griffin continued consideringly. 'But Izzy—well, Izzy is something else!' he murmured appreciatively.

The red colour that flooded her cheeks at this comment almost matched the colour of her hair. 'I thought we'd agreed never to refer to that again!' she bit out stiffly.

He shrugged unconcernedly. 'That was before. Things are different now.'

'Not for me, they aren't,' Dora cut in sharply, her hands tightly gripping two books she had picked up to replace back on the shelf.

That green gaze swept scathingly over her appearance once again. 'Obviously not,' he derided, shaking his head reprovingly. 'Charles was my brother, Izzy, and as such I loved him but nevertheless I was also aware of his faults. And one thing I'm damned sure of—he was not the type of man to inspire a love that would result in a lifetime of mourning at his death!'

Dora gasped. 'You're so—'

'Good God, woman,' Griffin continued, as if she hadn't spoken, 'even my mother has picked herself up from the blow Charles's death was to her plans of continued glory for the family name! And we all know how determined she was that Charles should have a respectable marriage—so that he could follow our father into politics and eventually obtain a Knighthood!' Griffin's mouth twisted derisively at the latter.

But he was right, of course. Dora had always known of Margaret Sinclair's ambition for her eldest son to take over in the political arena where her late husband had left off after his death twenty years ago. And as the daughter of Professor Baxter, famous university lecturer until his retirement ten years ago, Dora had been the perfect choice as a wife for Charles.

Unfortunately Charles had been killed in a car accident ten months ago, and all of Margaret's plans with him. Because even if Griffin Sinclair had been in the least bit interested in politics—which he most assuredly wasn't!—he was not a man, at aged thirty-four, to be moulded into anyone's else's ambitions, and least of all those of his mother!

'Something else I'm damned sure of,' Griffin continued, his eyes glittering. 'If the boot had been on the other foot— if you had been the one to die in that crash instead of him— Charles wouldn't still be mourning you! After a period of grief, followed by a respectable time-lapse, he would have been looking around for your replacement! Or my mother would—so that he could get on with his career!'

Dora knew that he was right about that too, her face pale now at the deliberate cruelty of his words.

'And how about you?' Griffin challenged. 'Hasn't your father found you another rising star yet, who can be moulded into a suitable son-in-law for him?'

Dora thought briefly of Sam, a doctor she had seen several times during the last few months, and knew that he didn't fit that description at all. Sam was dedicated enough; it was just that Dora didn't feel that way about him. And her father, she knew, on the one occasion he'd happened to meet Sam, hadn't been impressed.

'You know...' Griffin shook his head disgustedly, his smile humourless now. 'I always thought, with both their partners passed away, your father and my mother should have been the ones to marry each other—they're both ruthless, conniving, manipulative—'

'My father died last week, Griffin,' Dora cut in flatly. 'That's the reason I'm wearing black.'

He looked stunned for a moment, and then his mouth twisted wryly. 'Are you sure? Did you double check before they—?'

'Griffin!' she gasped, incredulous at his complete lack of feeling for her loss, as well as the death of another human being. In their short acquaintance, Griffin had struck her as many things, but unfeeling wasn't one of them...

'His sort don't die, Izzy,' Griffin maintained grimly. 'They're usually stuffed and put on exhibition—'

'He wasn't a "sort", Griffin,' she bit out tautly. 'He was my father.'

'Oh, I know who he was, Izzy,' he dismissed scathingly, 'I also know what he was,' he added grimly.

She shook her head. 'I've never understood this dislike

you had for my father.' What had he ever done to Griffin? Except disapprove of the younger man's whole lifestyle, of course!

Griffin was everything her father despised in a man: no permanent home, a job that he did if and when he felt like it—and Dora would be surprised if he even so much as possessed a suit! And as for that overlong hair—! No, Griffin wasn't a man her father could ever have approved of. But she had never quite understood why Griffin felt the same aversion towards her father... Maybe it was the reverse, and Griffin had despised her father's own respectable lifestyle? Whatever it was, the two men had heartily disliked each other from the moment they had been introduced.

'I realise that,' Griffin answered harshly. 'And I'm not about to be the one to shatter your illusions about him!'

She sighed. 'Griffin, when you arrived you said you had just called in to do something,' she reminded him firmly. 'Perhaps you would like to tell me what that "something" was, and then I can get on with my work?' She looked at him with steady grey eyes.

He looked about them pointedly at the bookcases of mainly leather-bound books. 'Not exactly bursting over with customers, are you,' he said dryly. 'What are you going to do with this place now that your father is gone? Sell it, I suppose.' He nodded in answer to his own statement. 'There can't be too much call—'

'I have no intention of selling this shop,' Dora burst out indignantly. 'I—have plans of my own. Changes in mind,' she added guardedly.

It still sounded more than a little disrespectful to talk of making changes in the shop which had been her father's work for the last ten years of his life when he had only been dead for ten days.

Her father had been—difficult; she acknowledged that. Since her mother had died, ten years ago, when Dora was sixteen and studying for her A levels, it had been just the two of them. And, once her A levels had been completed and attained, Dora had spent her time taking care of their home and helping her father in the shop, putting her own plans for going to university on hold.

Until her father no longer needed her, she had told herself at the time, not realising that that time would never come. Her father's health hadn't been particularly good after the death of Dora's mother; his heart-attack ten days ago had been devastating, but not exactly unexpected.

So now, at twenty-six, Dora was at last free to pursue her own aborted plans. But after all this time she felt it was too late. She had the house, and this shop, and had every intention of making something of her life. Despite Griffin Sinclair's derision!

He really was the most incredible man. It seemed he abided by none of the conventions that most other people lived by. His remarks concerning her father's death, for example, had been disgraceful.

Oh, Dora accepted there had been no love lost between the two men, her father considering the younger man to be a Bohemian reprobate while Griffin had believed her father to be—what had he called him earlier?—ruthless, conniving and manipulative.

Dora didn't completely agree with either of those opinions, but she had been left in no doubt that the two men disliked each other intensely.

And as for Griffin's reference to 'Izzy'…! That wasn't just something they had agreed never to talk about; it was something she preferred not to even think about, either!

'What sort of "plans"?' Griffin was watching her with

narrowed eyes. 'Don't tell me you're actually going to drag this place into the twentieth century?'

He could mock all he liked, but her plans were her business, and she wasn't about to discuss them with him. Griffin was the last person she would tell her plans to!

'I know this is difficult for you to believe, Griffin,' she told him tauntingly, 'but not everyone wants to travel the world, calling no place home, living out of a suitcase—by the way, what could possibly be important enough to have brought you home this time?' she added pointedly.

His mouth had tightened grimly at her deliberate barbs. And, in truth, she wasn't being exactly fair. The last she had heard of Griffin he'd had an apartment in London he called 'home', and when he 'lived out of a suitcase' it was usually in first-class hotels. And as for 'travelling the world', that was Griffin's job; the travel books he wrote after making those trips were highly successful, being amusing as well as informative.

Not that there was a copy of any of those books in this shop. Her father had considered Griffin's writing to be too light and frivolous to be taken seriously, let alone take up any space on his shelves! Once Dora had picked up a copy of one of his books at a hotel she'd stayed in on a business trip for her father. She'd found that Griffin's personality came through in every word; concise, humorous, derisive, but with warmth and charm also apparent if he had particularly liked the place he was writing about.

'Family crisis,' he abruptly answered her mocking question. 'Which brings me to— Aha,' he murmured softly as the bell pealed over the door as it was opened once again. 'I'll browse through the books and try to look like another customer,' he told Dora conspiratorially. 'That way it will look as if you have a rush on!'

Dora had trouble keeping her face straight as that was

exactly what he proceeded to do. The woman who'd entered the shop, probably aged somewhere in her sixties, glanced across at Griffin as he began to amass a pile of books in his arms. Books, Dora was sure, that he chose from the shelves at random, and was convinced of the fact when she saw him put a copy of a book about the *Titanic* on the pile.

The elderly lady's own attention seemed to be only half on the row of books she was perusing too, her glances in Griffin's direction becoming more and more frequent as the minutes ticked by. Griffin pointedly ignored her glances, his attention seeming enrapt now on a shelf of books on prehistoric animals!

It was almost Dora's undoing when he glanced across at her sideways, waited until the other woman wasn't looking at him, and gave Dora a knowing wink!

She gave him a reproving frown. Dreadful man! His irreverence—in any situation—was unbelievable!

'I say, miss.' the elderly lady had now sidled up to her, talking to her in a whisper. 'That young man over there.' She nodded in Griffin's direction.

'Young man'? At age thirty-four, Griffin hardly fitted that description! But with a definite lack of any other young men in the vicinity...

'Yes?' Dora prompted attentively.

'He looks very like Griffin Sinclair,' she told Dora avidly. 'You know, the man who does those travel programmes on the television,' she prompted at Dora's blank look. 'Do you suppose it could be him?' she added excitedly, looking quite youthfully flushed at the idea it just might be Griffin Sinclair.

As Dora knew only too well, it definitely was him. But it was the first she had heard of him being involved in a television programme. Not that that was exactly surprising;

they didn't possess a television at home for her to have seen him on. Her father had never liked that form of entertainment, and preferred to listen to the radio if he bothered with anything at all. Or rather——he had…

'Why don't you go and ask him?' Dora suggested lightly, looking across at Griffin with new eyes.

He would be good on television, Dora thought to herself. He had the looks and presence to carry off such a role. And if this elderly lady's reaction to him was anything to go by, he obviously had quite a female following of the programme, at least!

'Do you think I should?' The woman gave another nervous but also coy look in Griffin's direction.

Dora definitely thought that she should——if only so that she could witness his reaction to the obvious admiration this woman had for him.

'I'm sure you should,' she encouraged lightly.

'You don't think he would be offended by a perfect stranger going up and talking to him in that way?' The woman looked quite concerned that he might be.

'How could he possibly be offended when you are obviously an admirer of his television programmes?' Dora was beginning to feel sorry for the woman now, and regretted her subterfuge in not owning up to being completely aware of Griffin's identity——if not the television programmes the woman was talking about.

'But if it isn't him——'

'I'm sure that it is.' Dora put a reassuring hand on the other woman's arm. 'Besides,' she added mischievously, 'I doubt that any man could look that much like him and not actually be him!' As she knew only too well herself, Griffin was a one-off, if only in his unorthodox ways.

The woman looked across at him with adoring eyes. 'He is rather unique, isn't he?' she sighed wistfully.

'Unique' described Griffin completely—at least, Dora had never met anyone remotely like him, either in looks or outspoken manner.

'Exactly,' she agreed with the other woman emphatically.

'I suppose you think I'm rather silly; I know that my husband does,' the elderly woman acknowledged ruefully. 'But the truth of the matter is, I absolutely adore novels that have swashbuckling pirates and rogues in, and Griffin Sinclair looks just like a modern-day version of one to me!'

Dora glanced across at him. The pile of books that he carried reached up to his cleanly shaven chin—she really wasn't that desperate to make a sale! But with his long blond hair, that ruggedly handsome face, and with his complete disregard for outward appearances, she had to admit he did look a bit like a modern-day pirate...!

'Come on.' She put her hand lightly in the crook of the other woman's arm. 'We'll go and face this particular pirate together.' It was the least she could do after not being completely honest with this woman from the outset.

Dora was sure Griffin was well aware of the two women approaching him, but he continued to maintain his interest in the shelves in front of him.

'Mr Sinclair?' Dora tilted her head questioningly in front of him. 'This lady is a fan of yours, and would like to say hello.'

Was it her imagination or did he raise mocking brows in her direction before placing his pile of books down on the table beside him and turning the warmth of his charm on to his fan?

No, Dora decided wryly as she walked away and left the two of them to their conversation—gushing on the woman's part, huskily warm on Griffin's—she hadn't imagined that mockery at all. She didn't doubt for a minute that Griffin knew damn well that until the woman had told her so a few minutes ago she had had no knowledge that Griffin did anything to merit having fans! He was well aware of the fact that the Baxter household did not possess a television, because of her father's aversion to them—and she would hardly have been out and purchased one in the ten days since his death.

Although, she acknowledged with a frown, just the sight and sound of one might have been preferable to the silence that had fallen over the house in the last week. Not that her father had been a great conversationalist; he'd usually been busy either reading one of his beloved books or restoring one, a hobby that had become a profession over the last few years. But just knowing the house was empty, apart from herself, had made the silence seem all the more oppressive...

'—so kind of you, Mr Sinclair.'

Dora was brought back to an awareness of her surroundings by the elderly woman's gushing thanks.

'I'll treasure it always!' she added breathlessly.

'It' was a book that Griffin had insisted on buying for the other woman, gallantly opening the door for her too, a couple of minutes later, so that she could leave.

'Take that look off your face, Izzy Baxter,' Griffin drawled as he strolled back to where she sat behind the till. 'And don't say, What look?' He sat down on the edge of the desk. 'I know you too well to be in the least fooled by the innocent calm of your grey eyes!'

A shutter instantly came down over those 'calm grey eyes'. 'The truth of the matter is, Griffin,' she told him coolly, 'you don't know me at all!'

'I beg to differ—Izzy.' He raised one blond brow pointedly. 'But enough of that,' he dismissed lightly as she continued to look at him coldly. 'I bet that's the first time you've ever sold a biography of Dickens with a Griffin Sinclair autograph in the front of it!'

He hadn't? He couldn't have?

He had, she realised increduously as she saw the laughter in his eyes.

'I doubt that has increased its value,' she bit out waspishly.

'Ouch!' he murmured ruefully, his gaze lingering on her face. 'But it's good to see that, between the two of them, Charles and your father didn't knock all the spirit and fun out of you.' His expression was grim now, green eyes hard as the emeralds they resembled.

'Neither Charles or my father ever raised a hand to me,' she defended indignantly.

'They didn't need to,' Griffin scorned. 'Verbal abuse, in the form of constant put-downs in your case, can be as effective as a physical blow.'

Dora looked up at him wordlessly for several long seconds. But finally, seeing in his demeanour no hint of apology for what he'd just said, she turned away, before getting restlessly to her feet, needing to put some distance between the two of them.

'You're talking absolute nonsense,' she dismissed impatiently. 'Now I wish you would just state your reason for being here and then go.' Because, as always, he was shaking her natural calm. And after the recent strain, she needed to hold on to that. 'I'm sure your mother—for one—would not approve of your paying a visit to your brother's ex-fiancée!' Dora couldn't resist making a dig of her own; Margaret had always disapproved of Griffin's apparent familiarity with Dora in the past, and Dora had no reason to think it was any different now, even with Charles dead.

Griffin relaxed. 'I'm sure my mother's opinion—"for one"!—is of no interest to me!'

It had always amazed Dora in the past that it never *had* been of much interest to Griffin. Margaret Sinclair was tall and autocratic. Widowed while her children were all still quite young, she had taken over as the head of the family, seemingly without pause for mourning her husband's demise.

Charles, as the eldest son, had been groomed for the family's re-entry into the political arena his mother had loved so well. Charlotte, as the youngest child and only daughter, had been brought up to be a wife and mother— although she was neither of those things yet, as far as Dora was aware. Griffin, the second son and the middle child, was as different from his siblings as night was from day— his blond good looks against their darker colouring. He was also the rebel in the family, fitting into none of the careers Margaret would have liked him to follow.

It was a role, Dora had learnt after a very short acquaintance with the whole family, that Griffin nurtured and loved!

She gave him a rueful grimace. 'How has she taken to your television career?'

He gave her a sideways glance, green gaze openly laughing. 'What do you think?' he drawled mockingly.

'Oh, no.' Dora laughed softly. 'You aren't going to draw me into that one!' Although she could well imagine how Margaret had reacted to her middle child being on public television in a programme that, knowing Griffin, would be slightly less than serious. But, as in the past, Dora had every intention of keeping well out of the feud that existed between Griffin and his mother. Anyone caught in the middle of that animosity was likely to get trampled underfoot by one or both of them!

'She's horrified.' Griffin cheerfully confirmed Dora's suspicions, at the same time giving the impression—once again!—that his mother's opinion was of no interest to him. 'In fact,' he continued dryly, 'she was so angry with me when the first programme was televised that she didn't speak to me for a month. That was the most peaceful month of my life!' he added with feeling.

Dora gave another laugh, realising even as she did so that it was the first time for a very long time she had found anything to laugh about...

She sobered, feeling almost guilty at her humour now, with her father only dead a matter of days. And here, too, of all places, in the shop he had spent so much time in.

'And yet,' Dora murmured softly, 'it's you who she called when there was a family crisis.' This last was said half questioningly; Margaret had always been so in control, so self-possessed, it was hard to imagine a situation she couldn't deal with herself.

Griffin shrugged. 'Mother hasn't been quite her—autocratic self since Charles's death.' He frowned, as if he had only just realised that particular fact for himself. 'In fact, it was that that caused the row between Mother and Charlotte.'

'Charles's death?' Dora looked at him sharply.

The two brothers hadn't always seen eye to eye, being far too different in outlook and temperament for that, but Margaret and Charlotte had both adored Charles; Dora couldn't imagine the two women arguing about him.

'The time-scale of it.' Griffin nodded grimly. 'Charlotte's fiancé, Stuart—I'm sure you remember him? Well, he's been offered a job in the States,' Griffin continued at her affirmative nod. 'Which he is due to start in a couple of months' time. Charlotte, quite naturally, wants to go with him.'

'And your mother isn't happy about the two of them

living together?' Dora nodded—although she still didn't see how that involved Charles.

Griffin gave a mischievous grin. 'She certainly wouldn't be happy if that were the case,' he acknowledged taunt-ingly. 'Although, at twenty-eight, Charlotte is old enough to make up her own mind how she wants to live her life! But, no, Charlotte and Stuart are going to do the decent thing and get married. It was the date Charlotte set for the wedding that caused the problem. Four weeks on Saturday,' he explained as Dora still looked confused. 'That way the two of them will be able to have a honeymoon before Stuart is due to start his new job.'

By which time Charles would only have been dead for eleven months... And, bearing in mind Griffin's earlier comment to her today about wearing black for a year, it all began to make perfect sense.

'Your mother believes the wedding date is disrespectful to Charles's memory,' she guessed knowingly.

Once again Griffin gave her that sideways glance. 'Don't tell me you agree with her?'

'No, of course I don't,' she answered impatiently. 'You have a very strange opinion of me, Griffin.' She frowned, remembering some of his earlier remarks concerning her father and Charles. 'I'm very pleased for Charlotte and Stuart.' She had always been very fond of the other couple; in fact Charlotte was the only member of the family that she had continued to see for coffee occasionally after Charles died.

'Because they're getting married—or because they're moving far away from my mother?' Griffin muttered grimly.

Dora shook her head at him. He really was the most disrespectful man! 'I'm sure your mother means well, Griffin,' she reasoned evasively; she had been more than aware, during her brief engagement to Charles, that Margaret would make a formidable mother-in-law…!

'Are you?' Griffin looked at her with narrowed eyes. 'I wish I had your confidence,' he added disgustedly. 'Whatever, the wedding is going ahead as planned in four weeks' time.'

'How did you manage that?' Dora wondered curiously. If his mother could stop speaking to him for a month simply because he appeared on public television in what she considered amounted to a role of entertainer, how much deeper would her response have been to Charlotte thwarting her wishes?

'Bribery and corruption,' Griffin bit out grimly. 'But it's done now, and—well, that's why I'm here today.' He searched in the pockets of his leather jacket. 'To personally bring you your wedding invitation. Sorry.' He grimaced as he finally found it. 'It seems to have got a bit crushed in my pocket.' He handed her the dog-eared envelope.

Dora looked blankly at the envelope, making no effort to take it. Her invitation? Not just to the wedding, but back into the midst of the Sinclair family…!

'It isn't going to bite,' Griffin mocked as he still held out the envelope.

She hadn't seen Charlotte for several months now, both of them having other commitments, otherwise she would probably already have known about the hastily arranged marriage. And it was very kind of the other woman to invite her to her wedding, but, in truth, Dora felt her own involvement with the Sinclair family had ended with Charles's death. And the way Griffin had just breezed in here today, on the basis of delivering this invitation, proved to her she was right to have made that decision!

She shook her head. 'I doubt I'll be able to make it.'

'Why not?'

She gave Griffin an irritated frown. 'In view of your mother's initial reaction to the wedding date, and the reason for it, I would have thought I was the last person she would expect to see there!'

He raised blond brows. 'Scared, Izzy?' he taunted.

'Don't be ridiculous, Griffin,' she snapped dismissively. 'I was trying to be sensitive to your mother's feelings.'

'In view of the fact that she is never "sensitive" to other people's feelings, I wouldn't bother!' He pushed himself up off the desk, instantly making the shop look small once again. 'Besides, now that we've settled her initial—misgivings, she's thrown herself into the wedding arrangements with a vengeance! Charlotte's "quiet wedding" has been turned into a social circus!' he explained disgustedly.

All the more reason, Dora would have thought, for her not to attend. Oh, she still had all the social attributes Charles—and his mother!—had found so suitable for her future role as Charles's wife: she found it easy to converse with people from all walks of life, on most subjects—themselves, she had learnt, was usually a pretty safe bet for most people!—she was attractive enough, in a quiet and unassuming way, and, best of all, she was sure, there was no hint of scandal attached to her name.

She just didn't particularly relish her role now as 'poor Charles's fiancée', the object of pitying curiosity. And surely her father's recent death was excuse enough not to accept.

'In view of the fact that none of the family were aware of your father's death, he was, of course, included in the invitation.' Griffin seemed to have read at least some of her thoughts. 'But don't give that another thought; it will be simple enough for you to come to the wedding as my partner for the day.'

Now Dora did stare at him. *His* partner? 'I don't think so, Griffin—'

'Well, I do,' he returned in a voice that brooked no argument. 'Now, could you ring through the sale of these books?' He indicated the pile he had accumulated when the elderly lady was in the shop, having put them down on the desk. 'I have another appointment in an hour.'

Dora frowned. 'Surely you don't really want all these books?'

He grimaced. 'As well as not talking to me for a month, my mother decided to clear out the bedroom she keeps for me at the house. The "clearing out" included throwing away a collection of classics I had had since I was a boy,' he told her grimly. 'I'm attempting to replace them.'

Mother and son never had really got on, Dora knew, but even so!

Griffin might dismiss his mother's behaviour now, but she was sure he had been far from pleased at the time. 'If you can remember some of the others that are still—missing, I might be able to get them for you,' she offered helpfully. Books had always been a big part of her own life, and she could imagine nothing more awful than losing any of the collection she had amassed over the years, and still read over and over.

'Thanks.' He nodded. 'I'll make a list and give it to you.'

She wished he wouldn't watch her so intently as she totalled up the books; he made her feel nervous, and she had trouble concentrating at all.

But he continued to watch her with those knowing green eyes, and it seemed to take her for ever to get through the twenty or so books he had picked up.

'You must have had quite a library,' she said lightly as she stacked them into carrier bags, having noted that some of them were copies of books she had in her own library at home.

'And there you were thinking I couldn't read!' he drawled mockingly.

'You're being ridiculous again.' She looked up at him with calm grey eyes, able to breathe again now that she knew he was on the point of leaving. 'I am aware of the fact that you've written several books of your own.'

His mouth twisted derisively. 'I'll lay odds on there not being any of them in here, though.' He looked about him pointedly.

She stiffed at his deliberate mockery. 'We do have travel books—'

'But not by Griffin Sinclair,' he said with certainty. 'Your father didn't approve of me any more than I liked him!'

He was right, of course; her father had never made any secret of his disapproval of Charles's 'disreputable' younger brother. Although Dora very much doubted the oversight had been deliberately because of who Griffin was; the shop simply didn't stock the sort of books Griffin had written.

'I told you I intend making changes,' she replied abruptly. 'And books written by well-known television personalities are sure to be good sellers,' she added teasingly.

'Very funny!' Griffin grimaced, picking up the two bags of books. 'I'll see you in four weeks' time, then.' He strode across the shop to the door. 'The wedding is at three o'clock, so I'll call for you at your home at about two o'clock.'

Then she would accompany him to his sister's wedding, as his partner...

'Oh, and Izzy...?' He paused at the open doorway.

She looked at him warily. 'Yes?'

He grinned at her obvious reluctance. 'Don't wear black, hmm? For one thing, it isn't an appropriate colour to wear to a wedding,' he continued before she could make any comment. 'And for another,' he added tauntingly, 'it doesn't suit you!'

Dora sank down weakly into her chair once Griffin had gone, closing the door softly behind him. Griffin Sinclair, she decided—and not for the first time!—was the most outrageous man she had ever had the misfortune to meet.

But how strange it was that the elderly lady had earlier likened him to a modern-day pirate, because when Dora had first met him he had seemed like a man from another time to her, too.

Of course, their surroundings had added to that illusion. At least, she had felt they did then, and she had made that excuse to herself since as a way of explaining her behaviour. Whatever the reason, she had allowed herself to be cast under some sort of spell. If only for a brief time...

CHAPTER TWO

THE prospective dealer, a man with a book for sale that her father had wanted, had sounded eccentric enough over the telephone, but when Dora had seen the Devon hotel he'd recommended for her overnight stay, she had known her business visit there was going to be a memorable one.

She could have had no idea as she walked into the entrance hall, past huge open oak doors, just how memorable it was going to be!

She had felt as if she'd stepped back through a time warp as she'd walked inside the hotel. Dungelly Court had been restored, it had said in the brochure she'd picked up just inside the door, as much as it was possible to its past glory. Old paintings and huge tapestries had adorned the deep purple walls, and ornate mirrors hung on those walls too, with a deep red carpet on the floor that should have clashed with the colour of the walls and yet somehow hadn't. And in the two rooms that had led directly off the hallway there had been fires lit in the massive grates, logs burning warmly. And welcomingly.

It had been unreal. *Surreal.*

'Someone will come and see to you shortly.'

Dora's overnight bag almost slipped from her fingers at the sound of that rich male voice. She looked cautiously into the deserted room to the right of the main doorway. At least, a room she had assumed to be deserted!

A man now stood to one side of the huge open fireplace, a man dressed completely in black, only the golden blondness of his long hair alleviating that impression of darkness.

26

Where he had come from, Dora had no idea, but she had been sure that when she'd glanced into the room a few moments ago it had been empty. The bar that stood at one end of the room was still closed at this time of the morning, the tables and chairs placed casually about the room were all empty too, although candles burned in holders on every tabletop, despite the earliness of the hour.

Her gaze returned nervously to the man. One of his hands rested on the huge wooden lintel above the fireplace. 'Where_is everyone?' Her voice sounded hushed and hollow.

Understandably so—not only did she seem to have stepped back in time, but she had done so with this blond giant of a man, who now stood looking at her with cool green eyes.

'Couldn't tell you.' The man shrugged dismissively. 'Do you have a room booked? They don't seem too busy at the moment so I don't think it will matter whether you have or not, but—'

'I booked,' Dora put in quickly. 'Miss Baxter.'

The man moved behind the bar, glancing in a red leather-bound book that lay open on its top. 'Yep.' He nodded. 'Miss I. Baxter.' He looked up at her with those compelling eyes. 'What does the ''I'' stand for?' He quirked one blond brow.

'Isadora,' she admitted reluctantly. 'But my family has always called me—'

'Izzy,' the man put in with satisfaction as he strolled back from behind the bar, seeming to savour the way the name rolled off his tongue. 'I like it.' He nodded, tilting his head to one side as he gave her a considering look. 'It suits you,' he finally murmured.

Finally, because Dora found she had been holding her breath as she waited for his next comment! And no one had ever called her Izzy...! It had always been Isadora if her parents were displeased with her, and Dora if they weren't. But, strangely enough, she found that she liked the name Izzy. It seemed to make her sound different, and, as such, was perfectly in harmony with the surreal quality of this country inn.

'Griffin Sinclair.' The man held out his hand, a hand that was cool and firm to the touch, the clasp firm, as Dora discovered when she touched it politely. 'I was named after my mother's least favourite uncle,' he added by way of explanation, grimacing his feelings about that. 'Least favourite, but the man with all the money,' he added dryly. 'Can I get you a drink while you're waiting?' he offered lightly.

Just listening to this man was like having arrows hurled in your direction. In his case they were arrows of information, but after Dora's long drive here, and the strangeness of her surroundings, her head was starting to spin!

'I'm so sorry.' She gave a wan smile. 'I didn't realise you worked here.'

'I don't,' he assured her cheerfully. 'I'm a guest too. But I would be happy to get you a drink.'

Dora frowned. This man had appeared as if from thin air, he chose to call her Izzy, when no one else ever had, he had been named Griffin after his mother's rich but disliked uncle, and he'd casually offered to get her a drink as if he owned the place, when in fact he was merely a guest, like herself!

She certainly didn't need a drink; in fact she already felt as if she were slightly drunk!

'I'll wait and have a coffee, thank you,' she replied somewhat dazedly, looking about her thoughtfully. 'Isn't it a little—odd, that there's no one here to book me in?' she murmured awkwardly.

'Part of the hotel's charm.' Griffin shrugged dismissively once again, sitting down on one of the high stools that stood in front of the bar. 'That's something you'll learn this place has by the barrel-load,' he added with satisfaction. 'Right down to its secret passage that leads down on to the beach. For the smugglers,' he added as she still looked blank. 'It used to be quite a lucrative business in these parts.'

Secret passage...? 'I don't suppose its source is in this room?' Dora wondered ruefully; after all, he had to have appeared in this room from somewhere!

Griffin grinned, obviously now guessing the reason for her initial discomfort. 'Behind the suit of armour.' He nodded towards the niche in the corner of the room where the armour stood on display. 'One of the panels moves. You go down a flight of stairs, and the passageway leads down to a cave that opens out on to the beach a quarter of a mile away.'

Not too keen on dark, confined spaces, Dora couldn't see herself ever making that particular trip, so he could have saved himself the explanation. Besides, she was only here overnight. She had her dealer to see later today, and then tomorrow morning she would be driving back to Hampshire, where she lived. Which didn't leave too much time for exploring secret passages and caves on to beaches—thank goodness!

'I don't—Good grief...!' Dora breathed in a panicked squeak as the biggest dog she had ever set eyes on stood calmly in the doorway. Dog? The huge grey beast looked more like a horse!

'Griffin!' She moved as quickly as she dared—just above a snail's pace!—and threw herself into the protection of Griffin's arms.

Yes, Griffin, at least, was very real! Dora could feel the hard warmth of his chest beneath her cheek, smell the male warmth of him. Yes, he might be real—but the rest of this was turning into a nightmare!

Griffin's arms moved comfortably about her at the same time as he began to chuckle, a huskily attractive sound that reverberated through his chest. 'It's only Derry,' he laughed softly. 'Admittedly, he looks rather fierce, but he's actually very gentle. In fact, a pussycat!'

A pussycat! The dog looked far from gentle as he surveyed the room with a steady gaze.

Even as Dora continued to look at him in horrified fascination the dog decided to stroll further into the room, walking over to the fire before dropping his huge weight down in front of it, his massive head coming down to rest on his front paws as he proceeded to gaze at the flames, totally ignoring the two humans in the room.

Although Dora had a feeling the dog wouldn't look quite so unconcerned if either of them should try to make a move. What sort of hotel was this?

She was very much afraid she would *have* to make a move of some sort. She still stood within the protective embrace of Griffin Sinclair. She was extremely conscious of the powerful warmth of his body, and could smell the male freshness of his aftershave, too, now. This man was a complete stranger to her; she *would* have to move!

But before she could do so a tall blonde woman, probably in her forties, strolled into the room. Everyone seemed to stroll in his hotel, Dora decided irritably; so much for efficiency of service. And yet everywhere looked neat and clean, and the fires were well tended—as were the extensive grounds outside.

Having already had the feeling that she'd stepped back in time, Dora was far from amused by the woman's opening remark!

'So you've found a friend to share your four-poster bed

after all, Griffin,' she drawled pleasantly, smiling warmly at Dora, pausing to stroke the Irish wolfhound's head absently before stepping lightly behind the bar. 'Can I get you both a drink? On the house, of course.'

Griffin chuckled again as Dora moved indignantly out of his arms, winking at her conspiratorially before turning back to face the other woman. 'This is Miss Izzy Baxter—your new paying guest!' he added, with obvious enjoyment at the mistake that had been made. 'And she's already turned down the suggestion of an alcoholic drink. Izzy, this is the lady who owns Dungelly Court—Fiona Madison.'

The two women looked at each other with new eyes; Fiona Madison taking on a more businesslike expression, Dora's frown deepening. Griffin had claimed to be a guest here too, but was he a paying one? He and Fiona Madison seemed extremely familiar with each other...

'Sorry about that, Izzy.' Fiona gave a dismissive laugh. 'I thought—well, never mind what I thought,' she said briskly as Dora continued to look at her coolly. 'Would you like to sign the register? And then I'll take you to your room. Have you had a very long journey?' she continued conversationally as Dora signed her name in the red leather book Griffin had looked in earlier.

A long journey? It felt, in these unreal surroundings, as if she had been travelling for years—backwards!

Fiona laughed again as she easily read Dora's slightly dazed expression. 'This place is something else, isn't it?' she acknowledged fondly. 'My late husband spent the last five years of his life lovingly restoring it,' she added wistfully.

Late husband? This beautiful woman, probably only forty-three or four, was a widow? Again Dora looked speculatively at Griffin Sinclair. Though the other woman's tone had borne no rancour minutes ago, when she'd made that remark about Griffin having found a friend to share his four-poster...

'He did a wonderful job of it,' Dora told the other woman politely. Mr Madison, whoever he might have been, had certainly fooled her when she'd arrived!

'Mmm,' the older woman acknowledged wistfully, definitely giving the impression she would rather have had her husband back at her side than all the visible charm he had returned to Dungelly Court. 'I'll show you to your room,' Fiona added lightly, coming out from behind the bar.

'See you later, Izzy,' Griffin Sinclair called after her, mockery edging his tone now—as if he had half guessed Dora's speculation concerning himself and Fiona Madison and was amused by it!

He *would* be, Dora decided crossly; the man seemed to laugh at everything—but especially at her!

And, considering she usually took life so seriously, never having time in her life for the air of frivolity Griffin Sinclair seemed to possess, she found the fact irksome to say the least.

'Perhaps we could have lunch together?' he called softly as Dora reached the doorway.

She turned slowly, not sure if he were talking to her or Fiona Madison. But Griffin appeared to be looking straight at her, one of those blond brows raised questioningly over green eyes.

Dora drew in a deep breath. 'I'm afraid I already have a luncheon appointment,' she was able to answer truthfully, and with not a little relief at having the prior engagement.

The hotel obviously wasn't particularly busy, and Griffin was as obviously bored with his own company, but Dora certainly wasn't going to provide him with his entertainment. Although part of her acknowledged that, with her initial reaction to him and this hotel, she'd probably already done that!

He looked unperturbed by her refusal. 'See you later, then.' He nodded dismissively, although his gaze remained on her as she left the room.

To Dora's further dismay the Irish wolfhound had stood up and now followed her and Fiona from the room. His head, when he raised it to look at her, was almost on a level with Dora's own. Her father had always been of the opinion that keeping cats and dogs as pets in the home was a sign of man's weakness, so Dora hadn't grown up comfortable with either species, let alone one that looked as if it could devour her with one bite of those massive jaws!

'Derry is completely harmless,' Fiona assured her as Dora gave worried glances towards the following dog. 'He wouldn't hurt a fly—would you, boy?' She gave the massive head an affectionate rub. 'You should see him with children.' Fiona shook her head ruefully. 'He rolls over and lets them tickle his tummy.'

Dora would as soon have Griffin Sinclair roll over and tickle his tummy as she would this huge dog! 'How nice,' she murmured weakly.

All thought of the dog and Griffin Sinclair fled her mind as Fiona took her up a short flight of stairs and unlocked the door at the top, throwing it open so that Dora could view her room.

A room it certainly was, but like no other hotel room Dora had ever seen. Here the walls were painted yellow, but still with that rich red carpet on the floor; there were more tapestries on the walls, and another fireplace, but filled with a huge vase of dried flowers this time, and several pieces of antique furniture. Against the farthest wall stood a four-poster bed.

Dora's cheeks flushed fiery red as she recalled Fiona's

earlier remark to Griffin concerning the four-poster in his own room...

'We only have ten guestrooms,' Fiona told her lightly. 'The restaurant is our main attraction—a carvery, of course,' she added ruefully. 'Shall I reserve a table for you for dinner this evening?' she enquired pleasantly.

Dora was still disoriented, and this bedroom only added to the illusion. 'Please,' she accepted gratefully, her attention caught and held by the tapestry over the unlit fireplace. A lion and a unicorn... How appropriate! 'I collect books and figures of unicorns myself,' she told Fiona Madison somewhat shyly as the other woman saw her fascination with the tapestry.

It was a subject Dora and her father totally disagreed on, her father claiming the beast was totally mythical, and therefore foolish, and so by tacit agreement it was something the two of them never referred to. Dora's collection was kept in her bedroom, where only she could see it.

'Then this room was obviously meant for you to stay in.' The other woman squeezed her arm as if in understanding. 'Make yourself at home,' she added warmly. 'And if you need anything, just come down and ask—I promise you that someone will be in the bar,' she added ruefully, after the earlier oversight. 'There are no telephones in the rooms, I'm afraid. They are totally destructive to any peace and quiet our guests might desire—as well as being totally out of keeping with the twelfth century!'

They hadn't had radiators in the twelfth century either, or running water in the bathrooms—in fact, they probably hadn't even had bathrooms in the house!

But as Dora dropped down wearily on to the four-poster bed once the other woman had left, she found she didn't particularly care about the lack of a telephone. The complete silence in the room, apart from the sound of birds singing outside in the garden, only added to the mystery that was fast becoming Dungelly Court.

In fact, the peace and quiet, and the total lack of formality from the owner of the hotel, filled Dora with a lethargy of her own, making her feel somewhat reluctant to step outside and let the real world in again.

But she did have that appointment for lunch with her father's dealer. She was sure she would feel refreshed once she had indulged in the cup of coffee she had mentioned earlier. A shower and a change of clothes would complete the transformation, and then perhaps she would be able to view this place with the detachment she now felt was necessary.

Griffin Sinclair, she readily admitted to herself, was part of what she needed to detach herself from! He was aged, she guessed, in his early thirties, and the shoulder length of his hair was unfashionable to say the least—although Griffin's confident air seemed to state he didn't give a damn for fashion! He'd certainly made an impression on her. If only for the fact that after only a few minutes' acquaintance he had asked her to join him for lunch!

Colour heated Dora's cheeks as she remembered the way he had looked at her. She'd never had any illusions concerning the way she looked: a little over five feet in height, slender, with a pale complexion and vibrant red hair. Griffin Sinclair, she decided, must either be very bored to have asked her to join him for lunch, or else he had been playing with her. She was not too happy with either possible explanation!

Forget Griffin Sinclair, she told herself half an hour later as she drove away from the hotel to go to her appointment; with any luck he might have checked out by the time she returned.

* * *

He hadn't booked out. In fact, far from it!

The bar, Dora discovered when she wandered downstairs shortly before eight o'clock that evening—having taken a slight detour on the way when she had inadvertently turned left instead of right at the bottom of the stairs!—in contrast to the morning, when she had arrived, was absolutely packed with people. So much so that Dora could hardly see the bar itself, let alone find a seat. The fire was totally hidden by the sea of people standing in front of its warmth, although that heat could still be felt even in the doorway, making Dora glad she had chosen to wear a silk cream blouse over a calf-length black skirt.

'Our table is through here.'

Dora looked up in time to recognise Griffin Sinclair before her arm was taken in his firm grasp as he led the way through the maze of small dining rooms that seemed to make up most of the lower floor of the hotel, warmly inviting rooms, with only three or four tables in each, log fires burning in the hearths.

'As you can see, it's very busy here this evening.' Griffin stopped beside a table, holding back a chair for Dora to sit down. 'I assured Fiona we wouldn't in the least mind sharing a table rather than taking up two!'

Dora frowned at him. He had a damned cheek assuring Fiona of anything where she was concerned!

But there was no doubt that the restaurant *was* very busy; most of the people that had been in the bar drinking were now starting to drift in to sit at their tables.

'And sharing the bill, too?' Dora drawled as she finally sat down.

The room was illuminated by the fire and a dozen or so lit candles. Very romantic! And with a complete stranger, at that. She wouldn't say he was a 'perfect' stranger, because she had the feeling Griffin Sinclair was far from being that!

'That would be very ungentlemanly of me.' Griffin sat down opposite her, pouring her a glass of white wine from the bottle he must already have ordered for their table. 'And although my mother may feel that she failed with me in most things,' he added hardly, 'she did bring me up to be a gentleman.'

There was a slight edge to his voice as he spoke of his mother, as there had been earlier when he'd talked of being named after his great-uncle. Dora's own mother had been dead for eight years, and she still missed her quiet calm, her air of serenity, her sense of fun.

'In that case, I thank you for dinner.' She accepted his invitation—albeit a *fait accompli*!—with a gracious smile.

Griffin sat back in his chair, watching her. 'You look right in these surroundings, you know, Izzy,' he finally murmured.

Dora had been aware of his prolonged gaze, and now the hot colour entered her cheeks. She had never been what could be considered a fashionable dresser, preferring to wear what was comfortable or smart, and, in the case of the cream blouse and black skirt, she considered them to be both.

Her hair was freshly washed after her travelling and her business appointment, and fell softly to her shoulders; her make-up was light—a peach lipgloss on her lips, just a brush of mascara to darken her lashes and enhance the grey of her eyes.

In fact, she had been quite satisfied with her appearance before she'd left her bedroom a few minutes ago, but she realised that she probably wasn't sophisticated or beautiful enough for a man like Griffin Sinclair, that his taste would be for much more glamorous women than she could ever be.

'I meant that as a compliment, Izzy.' His husky voice interrupted her wandering thoughts. 'I've fallen in love with the charm of this place.' He looked about them comfortably. 'I only meant to stay overnight initially, but instead I've been here almost a week now!'

'Are you here on business, Griffin?' She deliberately chose to ignore what he considered his compliment—and the fact that he continued to call her Izzy when no one else ever did. The whole of her visit to this hotel was taking on a dream-like quality; he might as well become another part of it. And, actually, it was quite exciting to be someone other than Dora for a few hours in her life!

Not that there was anything particularly wrong with her life. She kept house for her father, and helped him in his bookshop throughout the week. It was just that the very fact of being called Izzy made her feel as if she were somehow different, no longer the shy, cautious little Dora. Or maybe it was as Griffin said: the charm of this country inn just seemed to take over...

He laughed softly. 'This is my business, Izzy. I write travel reviews,' he explained at her questioning look.

'For Sunday supplements, things like that?' She had never actually thought about the fact that the people who wrote those things had to actually stay in the places they wrote about. But of course they did. And Griffin was obviously one of the people who did that. They had travel books at the shop, of course, but not ones that involved visiting individual hotels and giving a rating on them.

'Things like that,' Griffin echoed dryly, with a mocking inclination of his head.

'How interesting.' She took a sip of her wine, finding it light and dry. Just the way she liked it...

Griffin burst out laughing, uncaring of the female heads that turned his way as he did so. 'Take my advice, Izzy, and never take up acting—you're lousy at it!'

'But surely it is interesting?' She hurriedly tried to rectify what he had obviously taken as an insult. This place, or being called Izzy, must be having a strange effect on her; she wasn't usually so outspoken! 'I've always wanted to travel,' she added wistfully, knowing that while she worked for her father she probably never would, other than on business trips like this one. And she only made those because her father now felt he was too old for making such long drives himself.

When she was younger Dora had imagined she would perhaps take a year out after finishing school and before taking up a course at university, but her mother's death, and the need for her at home, meant that that had never happened. And now, with her father and herself both working in the shop, they had necessarily to take separate holidays. Most of Dora's friends were now either married or had moved away from the area, and it didn't feel right, nor would it be as much fun, for her to travel on her own. And so her holidays were usually spent at home.

Although travelling for a living, while it might be fun to start with, must surely become boring after a while...

'It can be interesting.' Griffin shrugged. 'Although my family keep asking me when I'm going to get a "proper" job!'

From what Griffin had said about his family, his mother in particular, Dora had the feeling he was quite happy to continue as he was—if it managed to annoy his family at the same time as providing him with a living!

Dora couldn't imagine living with such tension between herself and the only living member of the family she had left: namely her father. She preferred life to run smoothly and comfortably, not to be in constant conflict with those around her. Griffin gave every impression of not giving a damn about who he upset!

Her mouth twisted wryly. 'I'm sure they must be proud of you.' After all, he must be quite good at what he did, otherwise he wouldn't still be in employment.

'And I'm damned sure they're no such thing!' he returned unconcernedly.

Dora took another sip of her wine. In fact, she seemed to sip rather a lot of wine during the next couple of hours as they enjoyed their meal, and Griffin ordered another bottle halfway through their main course.

Dora wasn't sure it was exactly prudent to drink any more wine, but she wasn't driving, and she really was quite enjoying herself. Griffin was genuinely interesting as he told her some of the funnier stories of his travels, and she didn't want to refuse the wine and so put a dampener on their evening. Even Derry, as he wandered about the place, didn't seem quite as big and frightening as he had earlier. In fact, he seemed to have decided he quite liked her, coming to lie on the carpeted floor at her feet.

'Five feet nothing, and yet you seem to have some sort of power over rogue males,' Griffin murmured thoughtfully.

Dora gave him a sharp look, searching for some sort of hidden meaning in his comment—or one that wasn't so hidden! There was no doubting that Griffin was male, a fact that her racing pulse had been telling her all evening, and as for rogue—he was the most unorthodox man she had ever met! He had made no effort to dress for dinner, and was still wearing his denims. He'd swapped his black tee shirt for a green one, which seemed to darken the colour of his eyes, adding to their enigmatic depth. Those eyes combined with that over-long blond hair made him very much a 'rogue male' himself. But perhaps that wasn't what he had meant...?

'It was exactly what I meant, Izzy.' He sat forward, his expression suddenly intense as he reached out and clasped one of her hands in his own. 'Where the hell did you come from?' he muttered grimly.

She swallowed hard. He was playing with her; he had to be. In fact, she had been wondering all evening why a man like him should choose to have dinner with someone as ordinary as herself. In the end she had decided he was having dinner with her because there was simply no one else here for him to have dinner with!

'Hampshire, actually.' She deliberately misunderstood him.

Oh, she was tempted, so very tempted—what woman wouldn't be?—to go along with his flirtation, just once in her life to forget—

But, no! She was Isadora Baxter—Dora, who had never been involved in a serious relationship in her life—and she was not about to jump into a flirtatious fling now with a man she had only met for the first time this morning. A man who was the complete opposite of everything she had ever looked for in a man. She wanted someone sober, hard-working—a son-in-law that would at last make her father proud of her.

Her father loved her, she knew that he did, it was just that he'd always wanted a son, and having another child had been an impossibility after Dora was born. So it had always been Dora's wish to give him the next best thing; a son-in-law he could be proud of. She knew he would be horrified at her attraction towards a man like Griffin Sinclair!

'Would you like coffee now, or shall we wait until after our walk?'

Walk? What walk? She didn't remember him mentioning the two of them going for a walk, let alone her own agreement to the idea. 'I—'

'It's a beautiful evening, Dora,' Griffin added encouragingly, standing up to pull back her chair for her.

Dora stood up. She was feeling too mellow—from drinking too much good wine, she freely admitted—to be bothered to argue the point. Besides, the night air might clear her head.

She shivered slightly as they got outside. 'I thought you said it was a beautiful evening,' she said ruefully.

'Beautiful doesn't necessarily mean warm!' he chuckled. 'Here.' He took off his jacket and draped it about her shoulders, lightly grasping her arm as they walked across the forecourt and into the gardens beyond.

Dora tried desperately not to react to the lightness of his touch, which wasn't very easy when wrapped in the warmth of his jacket; the material smelled of him, a mixture of maleness and his aftershave. It wasn't doing anything to clear her head, either!

She sat down at one of the picnic tables placed around the garden, lit by the lamps placed strategically to emphasise the flowers and topiary. Unfortunately for her already shaky senses, Griffin chose to sit down next to her, so close that the warmth of his breath stirred the hair at Dora's temple.

And yet she couldn't seem to move away. She seemed to be held there mesmerised by the dark intensity of his gaze. And so she used the only line of defence open to her—words!

'I suppose you're going to give the hotel a good write-up?' She hadn't meant to sound sarcastic, but even as she said the words she knew that she did.

Griffin tilted his head to one side. 'And just what do you mean by that?' he said mildly.

He knew exactly what she meant; he was just playing with her!

She could feel the hot colour of embarrassment in her cheeks. 'I just thought, being such a close friend of Fiona's...' she mumbled awkwardly.

'I knew what you meant, Izzy,' he drawled with amusement. 'I just wondered if you had nerve enough to say it!'

Her eyes flashed angrily now. 'Don't play games with me, Griffin—'

'Then don't jump to erroneous conclusions—Izzy,' he returned hardly. 'Fiona is a nice woman; *I* may deserve your derision, but I'm not sure she does!'

Wonderful. Now she felt really awful! But he was right. Her sarcasm hadn't been directed at the other woman but at this man at her side. Unfortunately, it had backfired on her...

'They *are* erroneous conclusions, Izzy,' Griffin murmured softly as he saw her dismay. 'Fiona was very much in love with her husband.'

But her husband was dead...

Besides, that explanation didn't rule out Griffin being attracted to the beautiful widow. And Griffin was a very attractive man—even if he did give the impression he didn't give a damn about anything or anyone!

She swallowed hard. 'Griffin—'

'Izzy...!' he murmured throatily, before kissing her!

And with a passion Dora had never known before!

One minute they were sitting side by side on the bench-seat, the next he had pulled her to her feet, his jacket falling unheeded to the ground by both of them as he moulded her body to his, his mouth laying claim to hers.

For there was no other way to describe the passionate

demand of Griffin's mouth against hers. No gentle caress, no searching for a response, simply taking. As if he had been aware of her compliance all along!

Had she been so obvious in her attraction towards this man? Had she shown from the first how bowled over she was by his rakish good-looks?

Worse, had Griffin taken one look at her, a single woman of twenty-four, not beautiful, but not plain either, and realised she would be an easy conquest for his undoubted charm?

Was that the reason he had so arrogantly arranged for the two of them to have dinner together this evening?

Dora wrenched away from him. 'That's enough, Griffin!' she told him coldly.

He kept his arms firmly about her waist. 'We've barely begun, Izzy,' he assured her huskily.

She swallowed hard, looking up at him in the glow of the garden lights. Lovemaking with this man, she knew, would be wild and beautiful—everything she had ever dreamed it to be. But he was a stranger, a man on the make—and not for love either!

'You're wrong, Griffin—we've finished!' she told him scornfully, pulling completely out of his arms, resisting the impulse to smooth down her hair where seconds ago his fingers had run through it. 'It's been a charming interlude—'

His expression hardened, his eyes glacial. 'Don't dismiss me like someone you just picked up for the evening.'

'Then don't treat me like someone *you* picked up for the evening, either!' she came back heatedly, her cheeks burning with humiliated colour. 'Dinner was enjoyable, the conversation fun—up to a point. But in the morning I go back to my own life, and you'll return to yours. Don't delude yourself into thinking this place is reality, Griffin!' She looked about them pointedly. Even the gardens seemed to have a magic quality to them now: the profusion of spring flowers, the shadowy corners a perfect foil for the house itself.

Griffin still looked down at her with narrowed eyes. 'And just what is your reality, Izzy?' he rasped. 'Is there a man already in your life? Someone you go back to tomorrow?'

Only her father. There didn't seem to be much time or space for other men in her life at the moment. Her last date had been over a year ago, and, as she recalled, that hadn't been too successful.

But that didn't mean she had ruled out the possibility of falling in love, of marrying, of having children. She was only twenty-four, and she had all those natural yearnings; she just hadn't found the right man to share them with yet.

But that didn't mean she would settle for indulging in meaningless affairs until she met the right man for her. And there was certainly no room in her life, even briefly, for a man like Griffin Sinclair!

She raised her head, meeting the angry challenge in his expression. 'Yes, there's a man in my life,' she told him curtly, forgiving herself for not being exactly truthful about the role that man had in her life. 'As I'm sure there are dozens of women in yours'!' she added insultingly.

'We weren't talking about me,' Griffin grated harshly.

'Of course not,' she scorned. 'I'm sure you never answer those sort of questions about yourself!' Her anger was bordering on tears now. Tears of dismay. At herself. For allowing Griffin to get even this close to her.

No doubt he would return to his own life eventually, and he wouldn't even remember meeting someone called Isadora Baxter.

She wasn't sure she would have the same success in

forgetting him. 'I should go back inside now,' she said haltingly.

'Should you?' He was angry himself now. 'Why?'

Because this man was disturbing her, was upsetting the even tenor of her life. She should never have agreed to have dinner with him.

'Because I have an early start in the morning!' she snapped, turning away.

And with each step she took she expected to find her arm grasped as Griffin turned her angrily back to face him.

It didn't happen...

By the time Dora reached the sanctuary of her bedroom she was shaking so badly she had to sit down on the side of the four-poster bed. What a fool she'd been. An absolute fool! Griffin Sinclair had just been teasing her after all.

Just how far had he been willing to take it...?

As far as she allowed it to go, Dora realised with a self-disgusted groan.

The sooner she left this hotel, and forgot she had ever met someone called Griffin Sinclair, the better it would be. Most definitely for her, at least.

How could she possibly have known at that time that within six months of her visit to Dungelly Court she would find the 'right man' for her; the man she was to marry, to have children with? And that he would turn out to be Griffin Sinclair's older brother, Charles!

CHAPTER THREE

'RELAX, for goodness' sake,' Griffin chided impatiently. 'We're going to a wedding—not an execution!'

Dora sat tensely beside him in the Jaguar sports car. He was right, they weren't going to an execution, but apart from the occasional coffee with Charlotte, and Griffin's unexpected visit to the shop four weeks ago, she hadn't seen any of the Sinclair family since Charles's funeral. And she had no idea how Margaret Sinclair was going to feel about her presence today. Dora had sent a formal acceptance of her invitation to the wedding, but there had been no response to that, either negatively or positively.

Time and time again in the last few weeks, since she had sent off her letter of acceptance, Dora had been on the point of picking up the telephone and telling Charlotte she couldn't be at the wedding after all. But while she had known Charlotte might accept her refusal, she had known that Griffin most certainly wouldn't. And the last thing she'd wanted was another personal call from him, either to the shop or her home. She didn't feel she'd handled his last visit too well, and she had known that her protestations about attending the wedding would be in vain, anyway; Griffin just refused to accept no for an answer!

And so she'd struggled through the last four weeks without telephoning Charlotte, had even taken Griffin's advice not to wear black today. Although she had changed her clothes several times, before settling for the tan-coloured dress matched with the cream jacket, leaving her hair loose about her shoulders and her make-up light.

47

She looked cool and elegant; she was definitely Isadora today. And with one look at Griffin in the formal morning suit as he'd stood on her doorstep twenty minutes ago, she'd known she *had* to be the 'cool' Isadora today!

'I'm sure it's going to be a wonderful day,' she said lightly in dismissive response to his impatient remark. 'Charlotte will make a beautiful bride.' Like all the Sinclair children, Charlotte was extremely attractive.

'It is, and she will,' Griffin returned dryly. 'Now, would you kindly stop digging your nails into the edge of your seat? You'll mark the leather!'

Dora instantly moved her hands self-consciously into her lap, shooting Griffin an irritated glance as he chuckled softly beside her. 'I'm just a little nervous...'

'I would never have guessed!' He grinned at her before turning his attention back to the road, driving the sports car with easy familiarity.

Dora hadn't known, when they were at Dungelly Court two years ago, what sort of car he drove, but it had come as no surprise to her, when she'd met him again almost a year later, to find that he opted for powerful sports cars.

Charles had driven a Jaguar saloon, much more in keeping with his own image as an up-and-coming politician...

'It's all right for you to laugh, Griffin.' She frowned across at him. 'Personally, I would rather be going to the dentist to have all my teeth extracted than going to this wedding!' Especially with you, she could have added, but didn't. Because she knew damn well that Griffin would try to make something of it if she did!

As far as the rest of the Sinclair family were concerned, including Charles when he was alive, she and Griffin had met for the first time the evening she'd been introduced to him as Charles's finacée. Not by word or deed had either of them ever betrayed the fact that they were already acquainted with each other.

It had been as if by unspoken agreement that the two of them had met that evening a year ago as if they were complete strangers. Although Dora had known by the determined glint in Griffin's eyes that he would have a lot more to say on the subject when they were alone together!

And he had; he'd been mockingly derisive of her choice of his brother for her future husband. Although, to give Griffin his due, he'd never told Charles, or any other member of his family as far as she was aware, that the two of them had once spent an enjoyable flirtatious evening together. Or that he had kissed her!

'Personally—' he grimaced now '—so would I! Weddings bring me out in an allergic rash!'

She had guessed that two years ago, had known then that Griffin wasn't the marrying kind. But she most certainly was; she'd always wanted a husband, and children of her own. Although she wasn't so sure that would ever happen now...

Griffin shrugged. 'Unfortunately someone has to give the bride away, and as I'm the only male in the family eligible to do that, I'm doing it!'

Dora's eyes widened in dismay at this statement. In all the days and weeks she'd been dreading attending this wedding, she hadn't considered that Griffin, as her partner for the day, wouldn't be at her side during the whole thing. But of course he was going to give the bride away; so where did that leave her, Dora, during the course of the ceremony, and indeed during the wedding reception afterwards?

'We're going to the house so that you can drive to the church in the car with my mother.' Griffin lightly answered her panicked thoughts. 'You're sitting next to her in the church, too.'

Dora swallowed hard, gripping her hands tightly together in her lap. This was just getting worse and worse by the minute!

'Let's face it,' Griffin added derisively at Dora's stunned silence, 'someone has to sit next to her!'

But why Dora?

Griffin might find all this very amusing, but Dora had only ever found Margaret Sinclair daunting, to say the least, even when she'd expected to be the other woman's daughter-in-law! As a complete outsider now that Charles was dead, she didn't stand a chance against the other woman's cold condescending manner.

'Does she know?' Dora prompted reluctantly. 'That I'm to be there at all, I mean?'

Griffin relaxed back in his car seat, long hands easily steering the wheel. 'Now would I be so unkind as not to have mentioned it?' he taunted. 'Unkind to you, I mean,' he added dryly.

'In a word—yes!' Dora came back knowingly. 'It's just the sort of thing that would appeal to your warped sense of humour!'

'My warped sense of humour?' He gave her a sardonic glance. 'Who was the one responsible for setting that elderly lady on me at the bookshop last month?'

Dora couldn't help smiling at the memory. 'I knew you could handle it,' she dismissed. 'If it hadn't been for the objection of her husband, I think she would have taken you home with her!'

'There was only one woman I would have consented to go home with that day—and you weren't asking! No, don't stop smiling, Izzy,' he instructed impatiently as she did exactly that. 'You have a lovely smile,' he continued chidingly. 'And there's no longer a reason why you can't smile at me,' he added huskily.

Now that Charles, her fiancé, was dead? But that had never been the reason she wouldn't smile on him in the past—she hadn't even known Charles when she and Griffin had first met. The truth of the matter was she and Griffin were too unalike; she was quiet and hard-working, while Griffin was wild and irresponsible.

She turned away to look out the side window of the car, although she actually saw none of the pleasant Hampshire countryside; she was too disturbed by Griffin's close proximity, and the things he'd just said, to be aware of anything else but him. And she didn't *want* to be aware of Griffin. Even if she had once—very briefly!—believed herself half in love with him!

'How are the alterations going at the shop?'

Dora looked at him blankly for several seconds, surprised—if somewhat relieved!—at the sudden change of subject. 'Slowly,' she finally answered him uncomfortably.

The shopfitters were due to come in next week, and she still felt nervous every time she thought of the changes she intended making there. Mainly because they were changes she knew her father, if he'd still been alive, would never have agreed to...

Griffin nodded—as if he understood only too well the reason for her nervousness. 'Have you bought yourself a television set yet?' he teased.

She'd been tempted, in the weeks since she had learnt that this man had his own television show. But, strangely enough, that was also the reason she had managed to resist the impulse. She'd made a fool of herself over Griffin once, and had been haunted by the man and his kisses for months afterwards; she did not intend doing it again—even by watching him on television alone in the privacy of her own home!

She had learnt, when she'd entered the Sinclair family as Charles's fiancée, that everything she had suspected about Griffin that evening at Dungelly Court—the women, the wild lifestyle—was true. Griffin was most definitely the black sheep of the family—everything she had ever shied away from, in fact. He was a womaniser, a wastrel, and had no use for his family whatsoever.

She had firmly pushed to the back of her mind the fact that he was also the most exciting man she'd ever met in her life!

'I start filming my second series next week,' Griffin informed her softly—seeming once again to be aware of at least some of her thoughts.

'That will be nice for you,' she said uninterestedly. 'And your mother...?' she added pointedly.

He laughed huskily. 'You never give an inch, do you, Izzy?' he said appreciatively. 'I'm not sure Charles really knew what he was getting when he became engaged to you!' He gave a rueful shake of his head.

Dora stiffened. 'I had every intention of being a good wife to him,' she returned stiltedly.

'Izzy, even the best intentions can fall far short of reality,' Griffin taunted.

'I have asked you repeatedly to stop calling me Izzy!' There were two angry spots of colour in her cheeks now. She was furious. Although she wasn't quite sure why. Because Griffin had mocked her ability to be a good wife to Charles? Or because she feared he might have been right...?

Charles had been everything she could ever have wished or hoped for in a future husband: good-looking, hardworking, ambitious. But, as a result, he had also lacked a little excitement. She had cared for Charles very much, and she'd been sure they would have a happy married life together. And her father had approved of him...

If Charles hadn't died, they would have been married by now. They might even have been expecting the child they had planned to have as soon as they were husband and wife...

Her anger faded as quickly as it had erupted, and she suddenly found herself on the brink of tears instead.

'What the hell—?' Griffin turned the car wheel sharply, bringing the car to a halt on the side of the road before turning in his seat to look at her. 'Why the hell are you crying, Izzy?' he rasped incredulously.

'Why do you think?' she cried accusingly. 'The man I was to have married hasn't been dead a year yet, and—'

'Tell me about it!' Griffin muttered disparagingly, obviously thinking of the battle they had had with his mother over the timing of Charlotte's wedding.

'And you as good as say I wouldn't have made him a good wife, anyway!' Dora continued, as if he hadn't interrupted her. 'Just what I wanted to hear, today of all days!' She began to cry in earnest now, although she was inwardly aware that there was more than a little self-pity in her tears.

A year ago she had been an engaged woman, on the brink of marriage herself. And her father had been alive then, too. In just eleven months she had lost the two most important men in her life.

And what did she have in their stead? This devil of a man who sat beside her now, a man who teased and tormented her at every opportunity!

Griffin's arms were about her now, as he pulled her to him and buried her face against his neck. 'All I was trying to say was that you can't *make* people happy, Izzy,' he told her gruffly. 'I wasn't getting at you; it was Charles's self-centred nature I was questioning. You— What did you say?' he prompted as she muttered something against the hard column of his throat.

'I said—' She raised her head to glare at him. 'I said...' Her words trailed off as she realised exactly how close they were, with Griffin looking down at her with protective tenderness. Neither was a quality she wanted to associate with this man, and especially not now!

She swallowed hard, her breath caught somewhere in her throat as she looked into the depths of those luminous eyes.

Griffin returned the intensity of her gaze, his face only inches away from hers. 'You know, Izzy,' he finally said huskily, 'when you're physically aroused, a black ring appears on the edge of the iris of your eyes. I wonder...' he added softly. 'I wonder if Charles ever knew that...?'

The full significance of his words took several seconds to penetrate her temporarily befuddled brain. But once they did she pulled angrily away from him, her tears forgotten as she glared the width of the car at him.

How dared he? How dared he imply that Charles had never seen her physically aroused? Griffin knew nothing of her relationship with Charles. *Nothing!*

She was filled with self-reproach for her moments of weakness. Griffin was a man who accepted no limits, no barriers, not even those of decency. She had been going to marry his brother, his brother who had died, and yet Griffin seemed to make such a mockery of it all.

She turned sharply away from his eyes. 'You aren't a nice man, Griffin,' she told him coldly, wishing he would restart the car now, so that they could be on their way.

To her relief that was exactly what he did, manoeuvring the car back into the flow of traffic before speaking again. 'I'm going to take your last remark as a compliment, Izzy,' he drawled.

He would!

She was twenty-six years old, and yet this man reduced her to the actions and thoughts of a juvenile!

She shook her head in self-disgust. 'Could we just call a truce for today, Griffin?' she said wearily.

'Truce?' He quirked one brow wryly, driving the car with his previous ease.

Dora sighed. 'As in pretending that we actually *like* each other!' This whole scenario was difficult enough, without having to deal with Griffin's taunts all day as well!

He shrugged. 'You can pretend if you have to, Izzy. As for me, I've always liked you.'

Always? As in from when they had first met at Dungelly Court...?

'Actually, that's not strictly true,' he added thoughtfully, causing Dora to look at him sharply. He looked grim. 'I didn't like you very much the day you were introduced to me as Charles' fiancée,' he explained reprovingly.

She grimaced. 'Not good enough, hmm?'

'Totally unsuitable,' Griffin snapped. 'Charles was just a younger version of your father—'

'Stop it, Griffin!' She cut in firmly—before he could launch into another round of insults concerning her father! Admittedly he had been a hard man, not given to shows of emotion where his only child was concerned, but he hadn't always been like that. When her mother had been alive the house had been full of love and laughter; it had only been after her premature death that Dora's father had seemed to close in on himself and become so unapproachable. 'I meant that I wasn't good enough for Charles,' she firmly corrected Griffin.

'He wasn't fit to kiss your shoes,' Griffin rasped harshly. 'Let alone the feet inside them!'

'I—'

'Why the hell is it that women invariably choose a replica of their father for their life partner?' he muttered, as if to himself. 'What was your mother like, Izzy?' He frowned.

'Griffin—'

'Come on, Izzy, humour me,' he encouraged lightly. 'Tell me about your mother.'

She drew in a sharp breath. Humouring him was definitely the right way to describe his request; her mother had been dead ten years now, and Dora still missed her...

'She was beautiful,' Dora told him.

'I already knew that bit,' he dismissed impatiently.

Her eyes were wide. 'How could you possibly—?'

'It's a sure fact that you didn't get your looks from your father!' he cut in scathingly. 'So consequently it has to have been your mother!'

Dora knew there was a compliment in that statement somewhere, no matter how aggressively it had been given, but there was also yet another insult towards her father...

'We'll have to save this conversation for another time,' Griffin muttered before she could form an answer. 'I hope you're ready for this,' he added grimly as he turned the Jaguar on to the long gravel driveway that led up to the Sinclair home.

It was a long, imposing drive, leading to an equally imposing house made of grey stone, its symmetrical windows looking out blankly at the extensive gardens.

And, no, Dora wasn't 'ready for this'; she wasn't sure she ever would be. She had found the Sinclair home, the Sinclair family, intimidating enough when she had come here as Charles's fiancée; as she wasn't sure under what circumstances she'd come here today, she found the whole concept terrifying!

Griffin glanced at her briefly, grinning grimly. 'Don't

worry, Izzy; she's my mother—and I don't want to see her, either!'

Dora gasped. 'I didn't say—'

'You couldn't see the expression on your face!' Griffin chuckled, parking the car before getting out to come round and open Dora's door for her. 'Just remember, you're doing this for Charlotte and Stuart,' he added seriously, taking a firm grip of her arm. 'My mother is totally irrelevant.'

Margaret Sinclair could never be classified as 'irrelevant'! And, when they entered the family sitting room a few minutes later, Dora knew today was going to be no exception.

The last eleven months had not been kind to Margaret, her elegant slenderness having become unattractively so, the cool beauty of her face now lined beneath the perfection of her make-up, the darkness of her hair sprinkled with grey.

But, even so, she was still every inch the matriarch as she lifted her cheek coolly for Griffin's punctilious if dutiful kiss, before turning her attention to Dora. Dora felt herself stiffen under that penetrating gaze.

'Dora,' Margaret greeted her, a sharp edge to her voice. 'How smart you look.'

A year ago Margaret would have made that remark and meant it about the woman she had approved of as a wife for her eldest son, having already assured herself before the engagement was announced that Dora's background was impeccable, her morals equally so, and that she brought no baggage along with her that could possibly damage Charles's political career.

But now the compliment didn't sound so much perfunctory as bordering on insulting. Because Dora had arrived with Griffin…? Or was it just that Margaret didn't like the pressure that had been brought to bear on her concerning today's wedding? Whichever it was, Dora felt more uncomfortable than ever.

'She was hardly likely to wear jeans, Mother!' Griffin was the one to answer impatiently, his hand still protective beneath Dora's elbow.

'Don't be ridiculous, Griffin,' his mother dismissed coldly. 'Well, more ridiculous than you usually are,' she added scathingly. 'I believe your sister is waiting for you in her bedroom,' she drawled uninterestedly. 'Dora will be perfectly safe here with me while you're gone,' she assured him mockingly as he made no move to leave the room. 'Oh, and, Griffin…' She called to him lightly as he turned to leave after giving Dora's arm an encouraging squeeze. 'You appear to have peach lipgloss on the collar of your shirt,' she informed him, her eyebrows raised as she looked pointedly at the remaining peach lipgloss on Dora's dismayed mouth. 'I should sponge that off before the wedding, if I were you,' she added icily.

The fiery colour had first flooded and then fled Dora's cheeks, so that she was now actually chalky white. What must Margaret be thinking of her?

Should she try to explain how her lipgloss came to be on Griffin's shirt collar? No, she immediately answered herself. Those sort of explanations were typical examples of the lady doth protest too much! It was probably best not to confirm or deny that the lipgloss was hers—even if Margaret knew perfectly well that it was.

And Griffin offered no help at all, winking across at her teasingly before going upstairs to Charlotte!

'So how are you, Dora?' Margaret turned her full attention on her once they were alone together. 'Please, do sit down,' she invited graciously. 'I was so sorry to hear about your father,' she added with genuine regret.

Dora didn't know which to do first: answer as to how

she was, sit down, or accept the other woman's condolences.

After a few moments' hesitation, she sat down, at the same time answering the other woman. 'I'm very well, thank you. And although my father's heart-attack was a shock, at least he didn't suffer months of illness.' Unlike her mother, whose months of suffering with cancer had reduced her to a shell of herself before she died.

Margaret sat down in the chair opposite her, crossing one slender knee over the other, the blue of her suit a perfect match for the colour of her eyes. 'You should have let us know, Dora,' she returned with light reproof. 'I was very fond of your father. I would have welcomed the opportunity to pay my last respects.'

And her father, Dora knew, had had nothing but admiration for this coolly controlled woman too; Griffin was right: their respective parents *had* a high regard for each other!

'It was all rather sudden' Dora excused. 'I wasn't— It was— To be perfectly honest, I'm not quite sure who did attend the funeral.' Not too many people, she acknowledged sadly. Her father had become rather reclusive after her mother's death, and, having taken early retirement from the university, he'd lost contact with most of his former colleagues as he'd become more and more immersed in his books.

'Of course not,' Margaret sympathised politely. 'I know how the shock of Charles's death affected me,' she added, emotion showing for once in her usual cool control.

Although the other woman didn't seem to give a thought to how Charles's death must have affected Dora!

But mother and son had always been very close, probably more so because Simon Sinclair had died when all the children were quite young, and Charles, as the eldest son, had effectively become the man of the house.

Dora had certainly been made aware, during her short engagement to Charles, that Margaret, having been the driving force so far behind Charles's political aspirations, wasn't going to take a back seat just because he would be married. They would all have been living in the same house together, too. Charles had not seen the necessity for the two of them to have a home of their own, not when this house was actually his, anyway. Dora hadn't been able to argue this last point, but she hadn't ever looked forward to moving into this house as Charles's wife…

And so she was sure that Charles's death *had* been a terrible shock for Margaret to come to terms with. Not only had she lost her son, but also her own place in political circles. For a second time…And it was a place Margaret had relished, one where she came truly alive. Dora was also sure that Griffin, with his wild, rebellious ways, could never take Charles's place as Margaret's favourite—even if he had wanted to, which Dora was sure he didn't!

'I suppose you've heard of Griffin's latest escapade?' Margaret bit out disgustedly, her eyes flashing deeply blue.

She made Griffin sound like a naughty little boy! And while that might be what he still seemed to his mother, that was the last thing Dora saw him as! Besides, she had no idea what escapade Margaret was referring to…

'Er—I'm not sure,' she answered evasively.

'Television!' Margaret spat the word out as if it were something slightly obscene that Griffin had become embroiled in, instead of a medium that reached millions of people in their homes every day. 'Uncle Griffin—his namesake, you know—would have been horrified!'

Griffin's namesake had been dead for over thirty years, and, from the little Dora had heard about the old reprobate from Charles and Charlotte, his great-nephew didn't only take after him in name! The difference being, Dora suspected, that Uncle Griffin had been so wealthy, so influential in the family, that his 'escapades' had been overlooked on that basis!

'I'm sure you're right,' Dora dismissed noncommittally.

After all, the opinion of a man who had been dead over thirty years was totally without relevance, anyway. In fact, she was sure that to the younger Griffin everyone else's opinion was irrelevant; he had certainly never tried to win any popularity contests within his family that she could see.

'Of course I'm right,' Margaret snapped scathingly. 'And once Griffin is living back here under my roof, I intend making sure that all that nonsense come to a halt,' she added with satisfaction.

Dora could only stare at the older woman. Griffin was coming back here to live? He and his mother couldn't be in the same room together without arguing, let alone live in the same house!

'Griffin is coming here to live...?' she murmured dazedly.

'Of course,' Margaret confirmed smugly. 'Didn't he tell you?'

There was no reason why Griffin should tell her anything, let alone where he did or did not intend to live! Although Margaret seemed to have a different impression of Dora's presence here today as Griffin's partner...

'Margaret, I think I should tell you that—'

'Izzy, Charlotte would be grateful if you would go up and help her put on her veil.' Griffin's voice cut coldly into the conversation as he walked back into the room unannounced, his narrowed gaze levelled warningly on his mother as he did so.

Dora was still reeling from the shock of hearing Griffin

intended moving back into this house to live with his mother, all too aware of the fact that it was something he had chosen not to do since he'd left university at aged twenty-one. Because mother and son simply did not get on... There was something very strange going on here, and Dora wasn't sure what it was...

But Griffin's remark shifted her attention away from that for the moment; Charlotte wanted her to go upstairs! What were Griffin and Charlotte trying to do to her between the two of them? Margaret was Charlotte's mother; Dora couldn't even be classed as a family friend any more. Surely Margaret should be the one to go upstairs and help her daughter?

'It's perfectly all right, Dora,' Margaret assured her caustically. 'Charlotte assured me over an hour ago that she is twenty-eight years old and, as such, perfectly capable of dressing herself!'

Except, apparently, for her veil. Dora inwardly cringed. Charlotte seemed to have decided Dora should help her with that!

She would be glad when today was over, Dora decided for what must have been the tenth time that day. Over and done with. The book closed.

And yet she still couldn't dismiss her feelings of surprise at Griffin's decision to move back to this house to live...

She stood up reluctantly. 'Does Charlotte still have the same bedroom?'

Griffin nodded abruptly, his expression unreadable. 'Top of the stairs, turn right.' He glanced at his wristwatch. 'And don't be too long; the cars are waiting outside.'

Dora hurried from the room, closing the door firmly behind her. From the stubborn expression on Griffin's face, and the triumphant one on Margaret's, she had the distinct feeling there was going to be an unpleasant verbal exchange between mother and son as soon as she was out of the room.

Griffin was moving back to live in this house…

It didn't make any sense to her. Oh, it was a magnificent house, there was no doubt about that, with its large rooms, the grand sweeping staircase she was now ascending, the carpets only the very best, the furniture all antique. It was just that Griffin had never made any secret of his dislike of his previous home, or the contempt he felt towards the childhood he had spent there.

So why was he moving back…?

Dora suddenly knew the answer to that question as Charlotte turned to greet her with a glowingly happy smile. Griffin had 'settled' the family crisis, he'd said, enabling Charlotte to have her happy wedding day. And he had done so by agreeing to come back here himself and live with their mother! Dora knew it as surely as if Griffin had told her it was so.

And she couldn't help wondering, after her recent conversation with Margaret and having seen that ambitious glint that had returned to Margaret's eyes, exactly what else Griffin might have agreed to…

Did Charlotte know of the sacrifice Griffin was making on her behalf?

Somehow Dora doubted that very much. Charlotte would never agree to her brother being manipulated in that way. Which meant that Griffin would never be the one to tell her what he was doing. And from Griffin's harshness towards his mother just now, when he'd walked back into the room and found Margaret discussing his move back here with Dora, she had feeling that Margaret's silence on the subject was another part of their bargain.

So why had Margaret told Dora? What could her motive possibly be for such a disclosure? Because one thing Dora had learnt a year ago—Margaret never did anything without a motive.

Dora never had been able to completely understand the older woman. She'd never been able to comprehend how a mother could favour one child, namely Charles, over her other two children.

But Margaret was even more incomprehensible to her now. Griffin was right, his mother had changed since Charles's death, and it wasn't only those obvious physical changes.

In the past, Margaret had put all her time and energy into forwarding Charles's political ambitions—Dora was aware herself that her engagement to Charles had only been countenanced because he'd already been thirty-four, and it had been time he'd settled down with a wife and family. But now, with Charles gone, Margaret seemed to have turned her attention on to her youngest son. Once again, Dora wondered just how far Margaret intended to push Griffin now that she finally had some influence over him. More to the point, how far was Griffin willing to go…?

But as she looked at Charlotte's beautiful face, Dora knew she would have to put these questioning thoughts to one side until later. At the moment Griffin seemed prepared to go to any extremes to see that his sister's wedding day went smoothly; it certainly wasn't up to Dora to cast any doubts over it for Charlotte.

'Dora!' Charlotte greeted her with warm pleasure, glowing in her white satin and lace wedding dress, her dark hair loose about her slender shoulders, her blue eyes dancing with the excitement of the day. Like all the Sinclair children, Charlotte was tall, having to bend down slightly as she gave Dora a hug. 'You look wonderful!' she told Dora admiringly as she took in Dora's elegant appearance.

'I think that's my line, Charlotte,' she told the other

woman dryly as they straightened away from each other.
'I'm so happy for you, Charlotte,' she said with genuine
warmth. She had always liked Charlotte, and tall, sandy-
haired Stuart was going to make her a wonderful husband.

Charlotte grimaced. 'I was starting to wonder if we
would ever make it this far! Mother has been— No.' She
put her hands up dismissively. 'Griffin says I'm to forget
about Mother and concentrate on being happy with Stuart—
and that's exactly what I intend to do. I'm so glad you
could come, though, Dora.' She smiled happily. 'Griffin
told me your sad news.' She squeezed Dora's arm in sympathy. 'So I appreciate your coming to the wedding even
more.'

'This is your wedding day, Charlotte,' she told the other
woman briskly. 'A day for only happy thoughts. So let's
see about this veil, hmm?'

Charlotte sat down in front of the mirror while Dora
arranged the fine lace on her head and about her shoulders.
'I could have done this myself, you know,' Charlotte told
her lightly. 'The truth of the matter is I wanted to talk to
you alone for a few minutes, and I doubt there will be time
for that later.'

Dora kept her expression deliberately bland. 'You
wanted to talk to me?'

Charlotte met her gaze steadily in the mirror. 'About
Griffin.' She nodded firmly, the beauty of her face showing
the same strength of character Griffin possessed.

Dora's hands trembled slightly on the lace of the veil.
'Griffin?' She tried to infuse light surprise into her voice—
but knew she failed miserably.

Why on earth should the other woman want to talk to
her about Griffin? As far as the Sinclair family were concerned, Griffin had always been just another member of

Charles's family to Dora. Unless Griffin had confided in his younger sister about their meeting two years ago...?

'I'm worried about him.' Charlotte nodded. 'Yes, I know—Griffin is quite capable of taking care of himself!' She laughed softly at Dora's scornful expression. 'But he and I have always been close—with Mother's attention focused on Charles, we had to take care of each other. Sorry, Dora.' She groaned as she realised what she had just said about Dora's dead fiancé. 'I know you were to have married Charles. It's just that—'

'I do understand, Charlotte.' And she did. In Margaret's eyes, her younger two children had been completely unimportant while Charles was alive.

But now that he was dead...?

Charlotte gave a rueful grimace. 'I really did forget for a moment. You see, Griffin has always liked you, and—'

'I thought you all did,' Dora cut in teasingly, having felt a jolt in her chest at Charlotte's words. Griffin didn't like her—he loved to torment and tease her. There was a world of difference between the two things.

'We do.' Charlotte laughed again at Dora's mockery. 'But Griffin has always particularly liked you—'

'I think you're imagining things, Charlotte,' she told the other woman briskly.

Charlotte continued to meet her gaze steadily in the mirror. 'Griffin has always been my big, protective brother, Dora.' She spoke softly. 'I've always looked up to him, admired him, and I flatter myself that I know him. The night Charles introduced you to Griffin as his fiancée, Griffin looked as if someone had actually punched him! I've never asked him why, and he's never offered me an explanation, either. And I'm not about to ask you now, so stop looking so worried!' she added gently as Dora would have spoken.

It would have done Charlotte no good if she *had* decided to ask her; Dora had no intention of telling Griffin's sister, or indeed anyone else, that she and Griffin had looked stunned on that particular evening because the two of the had once indulged in a mild flirtation!

'Anyway,' Charlotte continued, her veil in place now, 'whether you accept it or not, Griffin has always liked you. Why else do you suppose he delivered your wedding invitation by hand, if not because he wanted an excuse to see you again?'

Dora had wondered the same thing herself for the last few weeks, and she hadn't been able to come up with a suitable explanation. But she certainly refused to accept the one Charlotte was offering! Charlotte was in love, about to be married, and everything and everyone was included in those heightened emotions.

'Perhaps he was trying to cut down on the cost of a postage stamp?' she offered teasingly.

'Dora—'

'Charlotte, it's ten to three, and you're to be married at three o'clock,' Dora cut in practically. 'Don't you think you should be concentrating on that, rather than imagining—?'

'Keep an eye on Griffin for me, Dora.' Charlotte stood up, turning to grasp Dora's hands tightly in hers as she looked down at her imploringly. 'I know.' She shook her head ruefully. 'You don't think Griffin needs looking after. But I know my mother too well.' Her expression darkened. 'She's up to something. I just know she is!'

'Charlotte—'

'The thing is, Griffin believes he can handle her.' She shook her head distractedly. 'And maybe up to a point he can. But my mother has never really forgiven my father for dying, and so robbing her of her political status. She spent the next fifteen years grooming Charles for the same role, and you know what happened there!' Charlotte drew in a deep breath. 'She'll do anything, Dora, anything at all to try and get what she wants. And Griffin—'

'Charlotte, forget about your mother, stop worrying about Griffin, and just go off and get married! Griffin has about as much ambition to enter politics as I have!' she added teasingly as Charlotte still frowned.

But inside she didn't feel so confident. Could Charlotte be right about Margaret's plans for Griffin? Even if she was, there was no way Dora could see him doing what his mother wanted.

Not even for Charlotte...? she wondered uneasily. No, surely not!

'Look, if it makes you feel better,' she said as Charlotte still looked worried, 'I promise I'll keep an eye on Griffin for you.' And much good it would do her! Griffin was big enough to take care of himself. And if he even guessed at the things Charlotte had just said to her—!

But it was worth her promise just to see the way Charlotte cheered up, once again looking like the glowing bride.

Griffin was scowling darkly when she returned down the stairs, and his mother was coolly aloof, confirming the belief she'd had earlier that the two of them had been about to have an argument when she'd left them.

Was Margaret really planning to try and manipulate Griffin into politics...? It was the most ridiculous idea Dora had ever heard in her life.

Her breath caught in her throat as she saw Margaret was looking across the room at her, coldly, dispassionately, as if she were a bug the other woman would like to squash.

CHAPTER FOUR

'So what do you intend doing with your life now, Dora?'

Dora turned from looking out of the car window to the woman seated beside her on the back seat of the white limousine, once again struck by the deepened lines in Margaret's aristocratic face. And, from the way her hands were clasped tightly together on her lap, she was far from as relaxed as she wished to appear. Admittedly it was her only daughter's wedding day, but in the past Margaret had seemed to take most things in her stride. Obviously no more.

'I'm sorry?' Dora shook her head, giving a faint smile. 'I don't understand what you mean?' At the moment she was just getting on with her life one day at a time, dealing with individual problems as they presented themselves. Including today!

'It seems to me, my dear, that so far you've been very careless with the men in your life,' Margaret drawled, pleasantly enough. 'First dear Charles, and now your father... I merely wondered in which direction, and with whom, you intended going next?'

Charles dying in a car accident and her father from a heart-attack almost a year later were hardly her fault, let alone due to carelessness!

She looked searchingly at the other woman. Margaret's eyes glittered despite the pleasant smile that curved her lips. And Dora knew in that moment that somehow she had made an enemy of this woman; not a good idea in the circumstances. Hopefully it wouldn't be too long before they reached the church and she could at least escape the confines of this car!

It had been a mistake to come here today, as Dora had known it would be. Although not in quite the way she'd imagined... She had thought that Griffin would be her main problem today—and now all she wished was that he were here beside her instead of Margaret!

'By your presence here today, a Saturday,' Margaret continued in a bored voice, 'I take it you're no longer running the bookshop. So I—'

'Oh, but I am,' Dora put in with some relief. 'It's just that it's closed at the moment, for refurbishment.' That fact had effectively taken away her one valid argument for not being here today. And she hadn't been able to come up with another one that sounded in the least plausible. She wished now that she had just lied her way out of being here, and to hell with it!

'Really?' Margaret raised dark brows. 'What do you intend doing with it—turning it into a ladies' fashion shop—something like that?'

She drew in a deep breath at the other woman's unmistakable derision. 'I'm just redecorating,' she dismissed, relieved to see they were now approaching the church.

A pretty village church. The same church where she and Charles had planned on being married...

Strange, but she felt nothing as she looked at the grey stone building, the churchyard ablaze with spring flowers. Her brief relationship and engagement to Charles, had taken on a dream-like quality these last months, making her wonder if it had happened at all.

One look at Margaret's frosty expression as she looked at her told Dora that it certainly had! And, while the other woman might have once accepted her as her future daughter-in-law, as Charles's intended wife, she certainly didn't accept her presence here now. No doubt with Margaret's own initial objections to the wedding, because she felt the timing of it was disrespectful to Charles's memory, the other woman felt that Dora shouldn't be here for the same reason. And especially not with Griffin…!

'Come along, my dear.' Margaret had got out of the limousine and joined Dora on the pathway that led up to the church. 'We must show a united front,' she added disgustedly.

'United' was the last thing the two women were. Although to give Margaret her due, she gave every impression that that was exactly what they were, her arm linked with Dora's as she greeted people to the left and right of them as they strolled down the aisle on their way to their seat at the front of the church.

Dora was such a bundle of nerves by the time they reached their pew that she was just glad to be able to sit down, her legs shaking. She felt as if everyone were staring at her—and wondering what on earth she was doing here. It was a sure fact, despite her gracious introductions to old acquaintances, that Margaret would rather she were a hundred miles away from this particular spot.

And Dora was slowly coming to realise it had nothing to do with her once having been Charles' fiancée, that her antagonism was everything to do with Griffin having brought her here today. Charlotte was right; her mother was up to something. And at the moment Dora felt caught in the crossfire!

Charlotte looked stunning as she walked slowly down the aisle to her future husband, but it was to the man walking assuredly at her side that Dora's gaze drifted…

Griffin looked magnificent. Tall, blond, extremely powerful in the well-fitting morning suit, he was a fitting substitute for his late father.

And just as he and the bride drew level with the pew where Dora sat beside Margaret, he turned his head slightly and gave Dora a conspiratorial wink.

It happened so quickly and was so unexpected that for a moment Dora thought she must have imagined it. When she looked at Griffin again he gave no sign that he'd even glanced her way, let alone winked at her!

But then she saw Margaret's stony profile as the other woman stared rigidly ahead, and knew she'd imagined nothing...

Damn him! It was bad enough being here at all, without Griffin giving anyone—least of all his mother!—the impression he was, or ever had been, any more to her than Charles's younger brother. Because he hadn't, and never would be, despite those few brief hours they had spent together two years ago...

The marriage service seemed to go on for ever, and the photographs outside afterwards seemed even longer, all the guests milling around outside too as they watched the photographs being taken. Everyone looked happy, it seemed to Dora—it was only she who couldn't wait for an opportunity to slip away!

And when it came she took it, hurrying off down the pathway, lost amongst the rest of the guests making their way to their cars in preparation for driving to the reception at a local hotel.

'And just where do you think you're going?' Fingers closed implacably about one of Dora's arms even as the question was asked.

She turned to look up at Griffin, a look of desperation on her face. 'I've given Charlotte my best wishes, I've attended the wedding, and now I'm going home!'

Griffin's mouth tightened. 'I would never have thought you capable of having such bad manners as running out on me,' he taunted dryly. 'Although, as I remember,' he added tightly, 'you did it once before...'

'I...' Her protest died in her throat as she realised what 'once before' he was referring to.

He was talking of the morning she had left Dungelly Court two years ago. She had set her alarm for seven o'clock, had forgone breakfast so that she could check out by seven-thirty. She had hoped that by leaving that early she wouldn't run the risk of meeting Griffin Sinclair again. And she hadn't. She hadn't seen him again until six months later, when she had already become Charles's fiancée.

'Exactly,' Griffin said with satisfaction as the colour slowly heated her cheeks. 'That was bad enough, but today you're actually my official partner!'

'I am not,' she told him indignantly. 'I—'

'Who delivered your invitation?' Griffin arched blond eyebrows pointedly. 'Who brought you here?' he continued before she could answer.

'I—'

'Who are you sitting next to during the wedding meal?' he fired at her with satisfaction.

Dora looked up at him with unbelieving eyes. Not Griffin! She glanced across to where his mother now stood in conversation with Charlotte and Stuart. No wonder Margaret was so annoyed with her; she must believe she was after Griffin now!

'Forget about my mother,' he rasped as he followed her gaze, his hand tightening on her arm. 'I've never asked her permission or approval for anything I do—and I'm not about to start now!' he added harshly.

He might not be, but Dora was still very conscious of the things his mother had said to her in the car earlier...

'What is it?' Griffin demanded sharply, frowning darkly

as he saw the reluctance on her face. 'What has my mother been saying to you?' he demanded grimly.

She wasn't about to repeat what Margaret had said to her to anyone, let alone Griffin. She still had trouble herself coming to terms with what had almost amounted to an accusation from Margaret that Dora was a jinx upon the men she loved. It had been a vindictive and ridiculous accusation at the very least.

But perhaps to Margaret, who had loved her eldest son so much, it made perfect sense...

'Is your mother quite well, Griffin?' Dora ventured slowly, not sure what she was thinking, only that Margaret's behaviour wasn't completely rational.

But, after all, the only contact she'd had with Margaret in the past had been as Charles's future wife: a well-connected, quiet, unobtrusive young lady. In that guise she had been perfectly acceptable to Margaret and had been treated with graciousness and warmth. But perhaps Margaret's manner towards her today, when she saw Dora with Griffin, was the real Margaret...?

She shrugged. 'After all, it is her only daughter's wedding day. Your mother is probably just a little over-anxious with all the arrangements—'

'I asked what she's been saying to you, Izzy?' Griffin cut in forcefully. 'You may just as well tell me,' he advised as she still hesitated. 'Because if you don't, I'll just have to go and ask her.' He shrugged.

And Margaret would just make light of her remarks in the car, would probably imply that Dora was the one over-reacting. And maybe she was..

'It isn't important, Griffin. It really isn't,' she insisted firmly as he still scowled. 'And I think I should point out to you that we're causing a traffic-jam!' she added lightly.

The other guests were casting them curious glances as they passed, their conversation obviously intense.

Griffin barely glanced at the people strolling past. 'I don't give a damn—'

'But I do.' She put her hand in the crook of his arm, turning him so that they were walking in the same direction down the pathway as everyone else. 'And I'm not sure it's exactly proper for the man giving the bride away to wink at one of the congregation on his way past!' she teased, in the hope of changing the subject.

Griffin certainly did look less dour as he grinned down at her. 'When was I ever "proper"?'

Never. Not that she could remember, anyway. She had never known him to bring the same woman home twice during her engagement to Charles, and his manner, as a general rule, was disrespectful on almost every subject.

'Besides,' he added huskily, opening the car door for her with a flourish, 'I don't consider you just "one of the congregation"!'

She wasn't about to ask him what he considered her to be. She knew what his mother considered her to be, and for the moment that was enough.

'Oh, come on, Dora,' he encouraged softly as she made no effort to get into the car. 'If you stay you will at least save me from these eligible women my mother keeps thrusting at me in the hopes of finding me a "suitable" wife!'

Dora looked up at him blankly. His mother was trying to find him a wife? *Griffin?* What on earth for? But as Dora recalled what both Margaret and Charlotte had said earlier, she realised exactly why...

Griffin married? It should be laughable. And yet somehow, Dora realised, she didn't find it in the least funny...

She kept her face averted as she got into the back of the

white limousine. Although she turned to Griffin in surprise as, with his mother safely settled in the front seat, he climbed into the back of the car beside her!

A 'deathly silence' probably best described the atmosphere in the car on the way to the hotel where the reception was to be held. Margaret kept her face staring stonily ahead, and the brief glance Dora gave Griffin showed him grinning widely, obviously enjoying himself immensely.

He would, Dora acknowledged crossly. 'Light the blue touch-paper and stand well back' seemed to be the way Griffin operated. And her presence here today was certainly creating fireworks inside Margaret Sinclair, even if externally she was remaining coolly aloof.

Which led Dora to wonder if her presence here today, so obviously as Griffin's partner, was as accidental as it had at first appeared to be…

'Who is it you would like to hit?' Griffin had moved closer to her on the back seat of the car, whispering close to her ear now, his arm along the back of her seat as he looked down pointedly at her clenched fists in her lap.

'You!' she snapped back at him, conscious of his mother sitting only feet away. Although Margaret looked as if she were unaware of the two of them, acting deaf to their conversation, Dora felt sure that the other woman really wasn't.

'Me?' Griffin ducked back in surprise at the vehemence of her reply. 'What did I do?'

He just *was*, Dora realised frustratedly. And, while it might have hurt her slightly in the past that out of all the Sinclair family only Charlotte had kept in touch with her after Charles's death, Griffin was the last member of the family Dora wanted anything to do with. And after today that included Margaret as well!

'Never mind,' Dora muttered, ever conscious of the listening Margaret seated in the front of the car... 'We'll talk about it later,' she dismissed.

'Promises, promises,' Griffin murmured in a dry, disbelieving tone. 'I've already learnt—only too well!—that with you there isn't a "later"!'

She turned a furious grey gaze on him. 'Don't flirt with me, Griffin,' she breathed warningly. 'I'm not in the mood!'

He grinned unconcernedly. 'Save that excuse for when you're married,' he drawled suggestively.

Her indignant gasp was lost as they arrived outside the hotel, once again becoming caught up in the bustle of the other guests as they all surged into the reception area.

But that didn't stop her thoughts.

She had decided, after Charles's unexpected death, that she probably wouldn't ever be married, and men hadn't exactly been beating a path to her door over the last few months. There had been a few dinner dates with Sam, a man more interested in his career than a relationship, so those didn't really count.

Besides, women didn't *really* use that phrase 'I'm not in the mood' once they were married, did they...?

Charlotte and Stuart were already waiting to greet their guests as they entered the reception room. Dora stood in line next to Griffin as they gave the happy couple their good wishes.

'Don't let me keep you,' Dora told Griffin dismissively once they had moved further into the room and been given a glass of champagne to drink.

'You know, Izzy...' He gave her a considering look over the rim of his champagne glass. 'This eagerness you have to not spend time in my company could give me a complex!'

Dora sipped her champagne, looking curiously around the room and recognising several familiar faces. 'I doubt it,' she answered him dryly. 'Your ego is irrepressible! Besides which, I'm sure you must have other things you should be doing; you are part of the main wedding party, after all!'

'I've given my only sister away to a deserving man—I consider my duty done for the day,' Griffin told her grimly.

Dora gave him a searching look. 'Charlotte seems—concerned about you,' she ventured casually.

'I'm told it's a symptom of every newly married woman—they want to see everyone else as happy as they supposedly are!' he dismissed disgustedly.

'I think you're deliberately misunderstanding me, Griffin.' Dora returned his gaze steadily. 'Charlotte is obviously worried about you, and from some things your mother said to me earlier I think perhaps Charlotte is right to feel the way that she does.'

'You didn't say anything to Charlotte, did you?' Griffin put in sharply, tightly gripping the top of one of Dora's arms.

Luckily not the one holding the glass of champagne. Although Griffin didn't look as if he cared one way or the other, intent only on her answer.

'No, I didn't,' she answered him slowly. 'But I think perhaps *you* should have done so!'

He released Dora abruptly, turning away, looking across to where his sister was happily greeting her guests, her new husband at her side. 'The wedding today would never have taken place if Charlotte had guessed what my mother is up to,' he muttered grimly.

Dora wished she knew exactly *what* his mother was 'up to'. As it was, she just knew that Griffin had made some sort of deal with his mother, a deal which was obviously the reason Margaret had become so compliant about Charlotte's wedding.

.

But how was that deal going to affect Griffin's own life? And exactly what sort of deal was it? Moving back to live in the family home was obviously one condition, but what about the political career that had been hinted at, and the 'eligible women' his mother was pushing at him, obviously with a view to marriage? Was Griffin going to be agreeable to that too?

'Griffin—'

'Just leave it, Izzy,' he ordered abruptly. 'Let Charlotte have her day; I'll sort the other details out later.'

In other words, Izzy, mind your own damned business! And she was quite happy to do that. Except for that promise she had made to Charlotte...

'Your mother seems changed, Griffin.' Dora tried another approach. 'Since Charles's death, I mean.'

He shrugged. 'A salutary lesson for us all,' he rasped harshly. 'Never have favourites,' he explained scornfully. 'Because with Charlotte's marriage, and her subsequent move to the States, all my mother will have left is disappointing me!'

With his blond good-looks, and his successful career, Griffin was a son for any mother to be proud of. Except for Margaret, Dora acknowledged sadly.

Not that, being an only child, as Dora was, was necessarily an advantage. Her mother had always loved her, and been proud of her, but her father had wanted a son, and had never made any secret of the fact that he was disappointed with the one child the marriage had produced.

That disappointment had carried on throughout Dora's childhood and into her adult life, although there was no doubting her father had been suitably pleased when she'd become engaged to Charles, as the younger man had obviously been destined for political greatness.

But then Charles had died. And with his death Dora had again lost status in her father's eyes.

She had decided long ago that if she ever married and had children of her own she would love them for what they were, not for what they could have, or should have been.

'What are you thinking about now, Izzy?'

Dora looked up at Griffin dazedly for several seconds, having briefly forgotten where she was and who she was with. Not the thing to do when that person was Griffin!

'I was just thinking...' she moistened dry lips '...that parents have a lot to answer for!'

He laughed softly. 'I'm told it's the hardest job in the world—and it comes with little or no training!'

That was true. Who was to say that she would have made a good mother, either? She knew what not to do, but that didn't mean she knew how to do the right things. 'True,' she acknowledged ruefully. 'I hadn't quite thought of it that way before.'

'Put it down to lateral thinking,' Griffin dismissed. 'Aha, I believe the time has finally come for us all to sit down and eat.' He nodded across the room to where people were starting to take their places at the dining tables. 'And I meant what I said earlier, Izzy; you are sitting next to me!' He took a light grasp of her arm as he guided her to their table.

Dora had given up all idea of arguing with him. As long as she wasn't sitting next to his mother, she no longer cared where she sat.

Thankfully, Margaret was sitting on the other side of the main round table, next to her new son-in-law; Griffin was next to Charlotte, with Dora on Griffin's other side and one of Griffin's uncles—she couldn't remember which one— was sitting to her left.

So all she had to do now was eat her meal, make innocuous conversation occasionally with the uncle—and then perhaps Griffin would allow her to quietly leave. She was sure that as far as Margaret was concerned she had already long overstayed her welcome!

To Dora's surprise, it was quite a pleasant meal. The uncle—whose name was James—was the brother of Griffin's father, and he had a string of jokes with which he kept her entertained, the two of them actually having quite a good time together.

'He's sixty, and a grandfather,' Griffin leant over to whisper in her ear.

Dora gave him a reproving frown. Would he have preferred it if she had sat here and not spoken to anyone, and consequently had a miserable time?

'The grateful sort,' she came back sharply.

Now it was Griffin's turn to give a shout of laughter, his first during the wedding meal. 'At the risk of repeating myself—' he gave a rueful shake of his head '—I really do question whether or not Charles knew what he was getting when he became engaged to you! The little mouse not only has a damn great roar—she has claws too!'

Dora wasn't sure that accurately described her at all, but if Griffin thought so, then let him continue to do so. 'If you'll excuse me,' she said pointedly, before turning her attention back to his uncle and listening to yet another of his jokes—which *were* funny. But Dora could help thinking that she perhaps owed most of her frivolous mood to the champagne she was drinking rather than the company!

Even the speeches didn't seem as long and boring as they usually did at such occasions. Griffin made everyone laugh with tales of his sister during their childhood—everyone except Margaret, Dora noted; she continued to view everything and everyone through those cool blue eyes.

Margaret looked, Dora decided, like a woman shrewdly

assessing what changes she could make with Griffin and get away with. Once again Dora felt that surge of apprehension in the pit of her stomach.

Today's pleasantness was all a sham; both Griffin and his mother were just biding their time. What was really going on under the surface wouldn't become apparent until Charlotte was safely away on her honeymoon. And then, Dora had no doubts, the fireworks between mother and son would really begin.

'How did I do?'

She blinked across at Griffin, having totally missed the latter part of his speech, although from the applause and laughter that still ensued it had obviously been a great success.

'Very well,' she answered him brightly. 'Very funny,' she added confidently.

'Little liar,' he murmured good-humouredly, his smile meant for the other guests as they still looked at him. 'Remind me to ask you later what you were thinking about instead of listening to me!'

She would remind him of nothing of the sort! Hopefully, before 'later' arrived she would have managed to escape!

Although that didn't look like happening any time soon. The band was beginning to play as they all left the dining tables, and everyone looked on indulgently as Charlotte and Stuart took to the floor, the newly married couple gazing happily into each other's eyes.

As Dora watched them she could see exactly why Griffin had made the agreement with his mother—it was whether or not he would be able to live up to it that was the real problem!

'You've faded off again,' Griffin muttered impatiently at her side. 'Come on, let's dance—maybe that will hold your attention. I certainly don't seem able to!' he added disgustedly.

Oh, but he could. All too easily. And it was thoughts of him that were causing her to daydream.

But Dora didn't have time to dwell on that now. She'd been taken into Griffin's arms, while several other couples joined in the dancing, too, now that the happy couple had had their moment.

Dora had never danced with Griffin before, and found the experience nerve-racking, to say the least. He was too close, all of him: his thighs moving against hers, his chest against her breasts, his breath stirring the fiery tendrils of her hair...

'Don't fidget,' he murmured as she tried to put some distance between the two of them.

She wasn't fidgeting—she was trying to breathe!

Breathing was supposed to be an involuntary response, but for some reason her breath seemed to have got caught in her chest and wouldn't be moved.

Was it possible to die just from dancing too close to someone? At this moment, she quite believed it was!

Not Griffin! She couldn't be falling in love with Griffin! Oh, for a brief few hours two years ago she had allowed herself to be charmed by him, had felt decidedly reckless in doing so, but even then she had recognised that Griffin was a man who would never settle down with one woman—and especially not with one called Dora, who worked in a bookshop and lived at home with her father!

And so she'd played out their little charade, indulged in a light flirtation herself. Until she'd realised what dangerous ground she was stepping on. It was the only few hours of madness she'd ever known in her well-ordered existence. With a complete stranger. A man she'd believed she would never see again. But they *had* met again, and that time she had been the fiancée of his older brother.

To give Griffin his due, he'd played his part as Charles's younger brother very well. At least, she'd thought he had—until Charlotte's earlier remark... Dora couldn't say she'd noticed Griffin looking as if someone had just punched him when Charles had introduced the two of them, but Charlotte claimed that he had. And Dora had no reason to disbelieve her.

What had her own feelings been on that night over a year ago?

Horror. Fear. A dread that Griffin might claim he'd already met her. And disclose the circumstances...

But what else had she felt? How had she really felt at meeting Griffin again? The man who'd kissed her with such passion?

No!

A shutter came firmly down over anything else she might or might not have felt that evening. It served no purpose, only confused her—and at a time when she was trying, after years of living her life around her father's needs and wants, to make a life for herself. A life that certainly didn't include loving the disruptive Griffin Sinclair!

'What is it?' He frowned down at her as they still danced together. 'Your back stiffened and you suddenly grew two inches in height,' he explained ruefully at her questioning look.

Because she had come to a decision in those moments: neither Margaret Sinclair or Griffin were a part of her life. And Margaret's frostiness towards her, and Griffin himself, with his teasing and cajoling, would be of no consequence to Dora once today was over. The promise she had made Charlotte earlier was a complete waste of time; she never saw Griffin anyway, and he was quite capable of looking after himself!

'I remembered my father telling me not to slouch,' she dismissed with a shrug, the dance having come to an end— and her moments of madness. 'I think—'

'Ah, Griffin, here you are,' Margaret greeted him brightly as the couple left the dance floor.

Dora turned to look at the other woman, her eyes widening as she saw Margaret wasn't alone. Standing beside her was a tall, beautiful blonde woman, and Dora could feel the tension in Griffin's hand, where he had a light grasp of her elbow. Although he looked relaxed enough when she turned to glance at him...

'Griffin,' the blonde greeted him, with husky pleasure.

Was this one of the 'eligible women' his mother had found for him...?

'Griffin, you remember Amanda Adams?' his mother reminded him warmly.

'Of course.' Griffin nodded abruptly, his smile strained as he looked at the beautiful woman.

It *was* one of those women!

And Margaret, socially correct Margaret, was pointedly ignoring Dora as she stood at Griffin's side!

Which was telling enough in itself. Dora looked at Amanda Adams. Yes, she was beautiful enough: probably about Dora's own age, and yet possessed of a self-confidence that Dora could never hope to attain.

'Jeffrey Adams' daughter,' Margaret added pointedly.

Jeffrey Adams! The politician! A man predicted to be the next leader of his party, possibly the next Prime Minister!

'I thought the two of you might like to dance together,' Margaret told Griffin determinedly.

Now it was Dora's turn to stiffen. Margaret wasn't only

being socially incorrect now, she was being incredibly rude. Was Dora the only one to see that? Amanda Adams looked unconcerned. In fact she hadn't so much as glanced at Dora, either, her attention all fixed on Griffin! And Griffin—damn him!—now seemed absolutely mesmerised in return.

Well, if Griffin wanted to play into his mother's hands that was up to him; Dora certainly wasn't going to stand in his way! If a political career was what Margaret had in mind for Griffin, then the daughter of Jeffrey Adams would certainly be a 'suitable' wife for him!

'Please do,' Dora told Griffin tautly. 'I think I would like to sit down for a while anyway.'

'Well…if you're sure?' He barely glanced at her, returning Amanda's seductive smile.

She was sure. More than sure! The man was an idiot; he didn't deserve her help in evading his mother's machinations if he was stupid enough to fall straight into her trap!

'I'm sure,' she snapped, walking off and leaving them to it.

Although she couldn't resist glancing over at the dancing couple a few minutes later. The two of them were laughing together, Griffin obviously captivated by the willowy Amanda. A sideways glance in Margaret's direction showed the older woman watching them with a satisfied smile on her lips. Although her head went back challengingly as she saw Dora looking over at her.

Damn her! The sooner Dora escaped, leaving Griffin to get on with his flirting and saving Margaret her continued cold looks in Dora's direction, the better it would be for everyone! Surely Charlotte and Stuart would be leaving soon. One of the uncles had mentioned that the happy couple were booked on a late-night flight to Paris. And they would have to change and pick their luggage before then.

Dora breathed a sigh of relief when it was announced, ten minutes later, that the bride and groom would shortly be leaving. She joined the other guests near the doorway as they went to see them off. With any luck she would be able to slip away unobserved herself—more successfully than she'd managed earlier!—once they'd gone!

'Unobserved' was not quite the way she would have described herself a few seconds later, when the bouquet of yellow tea-roses landed in her arms!

Charlotte had followed the old tradition of throwing her bouquet, and when it had hurtled towards Dora she had instinctively reached out and caught it.

To Dora's consternation.

And Charlotte's obvious glee!

The other woman grinned as she gave Dora a brief wave in parting before disappearing out through the door with her new husband.

Dora gave a slightly sickly smile of embarrassment as she caught several smiles of approval directed at her from some of the other guests.

'An omen, Izzy. Let's hope, whoever he is, that you manage to hang on to this one!'

She turned sharply, the bouquet still in her hands, and found herself facing Griffin, and wasn't fooled for a moment by his innocent wide-eyed gaze. 'Charlotte's sense of humour is obviously as warped as yours!' she snapped. 'You're more likely to marry in the near future than I am,' she added scathingly, glancing across to where the beautiful blonde still watched him with avaricious eyes. 'Here.' Dora thrust the bouquet disgustedly towards Griffin. 'Give them to your friend!'

He shook his head, making no effort to take the roses from her. 'It doesn't work that way, Izzy. A secondhand bouquet doesn't mean anything,' he taunted. 'No, Izzy, I'm afraid you'll just have to face it—you are destined to be the next bride!'

'Like hell I am,' she muttered forcefully. 'I was going to marry Charles—'

'You would have made each other miserable,' he put in dismissively.

'You're insulting,' she gasped incredulously.

'You didn't love him.' Griffin shrugged. 'And I very much doubt Charles was capable of loving anyone more than he loved himself!'

'Of course I loved him!' she snapped impatiently, ignoring his remark about Charles; after all, she couldn't speak for anyone but herself. And Charles had said he loved her... 'That's the second time today you've said something like that.' She put the bouquet down on the table next to her. 'And, quite frankly, I find it rude. You have no right to— Why are you looking at me like that?' She frowned up at him suspiciously as he looked at her with one brow raised in sceptical mockery, his arms folded across his chest.

'Keep going, Izzy,' he drawled derisively. 'If you try hard enough, you might actually be able to work yourself up into a genuine state of agitation.'

'You're so insulting!' she bit out fiercely; she was going to knock that mocking smile off his arrogant face in a minute!

'You just said that,' he said dryly. 'Several times.'

'Then I obviously mean it.' Her eyes flashed deeply grey. 'I believe I've had quite enough of this wedding, Griffin. I've certainly had enough of you! And do not offer to take me home,' she warned in a dangerously soft voice. 'You've already caused me more than enough discomfort for one day!'

'I have no intention of offering to drive you home,'

Griffin said with amusement. 'No car, remember.' He shrugged. 'However, I could arrange a taxi for you if you really insist on leaving.'

'Oh, I insist! And I can get my own taxi, thank you, Griffin,' she told him impatiently. 'Now, if you will excuse me...?'

'Certainly.' He stepped back out of her way. 'Don't forget to say goodbye to my mother—after all, she is your hostess,' he called after her softly.

Dora could hear him chuckling softly to himself as she flinched slightly after his last mocking remark, but she kept on walking towards Margaret, where she stood across the room talking to her sister. Griffin was quite right; she would have to take her leave of his mother. But he wasn't right about her feelings for Charles; she had loved him. He had been everything any woman could possibly want in a future husband. But what would Griffin know of that?

'Leaving us so soon, Dora?' Margaret drawled pleasantly enough when Dora told her of her intention of leaving. 'Excuse us, Stella; I'll just walk outside with Dora,' she told her sister, once again linking her arm with Dora's in what looked like a friendly gesture.

Looked like, because from Margaret's earlier remarks Dora had no reason to believe the other woman felt in the least friendly towards her!

Margaret's friendly demeanour faded as soon as the two of them were outside in the hotel hallway. 'I just wanted to warn you not to get any ideas where Griffin is concerned,' she said, coming icily straight to the point. 'In other words, Dora, do not take the bouquet incident seriously. Especially in Griffin's direction,' she added grimly. 'I have plans of my own for Griffin—and they certainly do not include you!'

Dora stared at the other woman, stunned by the attack,

even though she had half been expecting it. It was the vit-
riol in the other woman's words and face that so surprised
her. No one had ever spoken to her like this before.

But she could guess at Margaret's plans for Griffin; if he
really were to enter the political arena at this stage of his
life he was going to need more than his mother's help to
do it, and being son-in-law of the next possible Prime
Minister would be guaranteed to give him that!

Margaret gave a smile that didn't reach the hardness of
her blue eyes. 'I'm sure you're wondering why, when I
found you suitable as a wife for Charles, I should be so
against your having any involvement with my younger
son,' she continued pleasantly. 'The truth of the matter is,
Dora, that I have someone eminently more suitable for
Griffin. I'm sure you're aware of exactly who Amanda
is…?'

And not only that. Dora had noticed several politicians
amongst the numerous guests, and had realised a few
minutes ago that Jeffrey Adams himself was one of them.
With the Sinclairs' family interest in politics, the presence
of the silver-haired politician wasn't of particular note. But
now Dora had seen his daughter, and realised Margaret's
intentions in that direction, his presence took on a much
more ominous quality. For Griffin, that was…

'I can see that you do,' Margaret continued smoothly,
after Dora's brief glimpse towards the middle-aged politician. 'Amanda is Jeffrey's youngest daughter. A late ad-
dition to his already grown family and the apple of his eye,'
she added with satisfaction.

And obviously the woman Margaret found 'eminently
more suitable' as a wife for Griffin…

But surely Margaret couldn't seriously hope to persuade
Griffin to take up politics where his father and Charles had
left off? The idea was ludicrous. Griffin didn't give a damn

what he said, or to whom he said it, and in politics that just wouldn't do!

Did Griffin have any idea of the extent of his mother's plans for his future? He knew that his mother was looking for a suitable wife for him, so he must know at least some of what she had in mind for him.

But, knowing Griffin, he believed he was more than capable of handling his mother. And any of her schemes. Although Griffin *had* seemed quite happy to flirt with the coy Amanda!

'I wish you luck,' Dora told the other woman quietly. 'As for me, I have my own plans for the future—and they don't include any of you!'

'I'm so glad you feel that way, my dear.' Margaret squeezed her arm. 'I'm sure it will be better for all of us if you stand by that decision.'

The woman was dangerous, Dora decided as she walked hurriedly away, not mistaking those last words for anything other than the threat they were. And not even a veiled one, at that.

Dora had meant what she said; she intended staying away from both Griffin and Margaret.

They were both dangerous.

But, as she'd realised earlier, when she'd been filled with jealousy at Griffin's obvious attraction to the beautiful Amanda, they were dangerous for very different reasons...

CHAPTER FIVE

'WHAT the hell—? Careful, Izzy!' Griffin rasped as the ladder she was standing on wobbled precariously.

Which, in the circumstances, wasn't surprising!

The last person she had expected—or wanted—to see was Griffin Sinclair. Besides, the shop was closed, and it clearly said so on the notice on the outside of the door. Yet Griffin never had taken too much notice of little facts like that!

'Come down from there,' he ordered as he came to stand at the bottom of the ladder. 'Then you can tell me exactly what you're supposed to be doing!' he added.

Dora bristled indignantly at his daring to tell her what to do, while at the same time realising the derision in his tone in the latter statement.

She was *supposed* to be painting the ceiling, but she accepted she had more paint on her than she managed to apply to the ceiling. Her denims and tee shirt were liberally sprinkled with the white paint, and her hair too, she didn't doubt. Whereas Griffin, also wearing faded denims, and a dark green tee shirt, looked as handsome as ever!

'I believe it is perfectly obvious what I'm doing, Griffin,' she snapped, deliberately making no effort to descend the ladder. She hadn't seen or heard from Griffin since the wedding six days ago—and she wished he weren't here now, either! But perhaps he had come to tell her of his engagement to the beautiful Amanda...?

Griffin gave her a considering look from mocking green eyes. 'Hmm,' he finally murmured thoughtfully. 'No,' he added a few seconds later, 'I really have no idea. Putting white streaks in your hair seems to be the obvious answer, but I would've thought you'd be better going to a hair-dresser and having that done professionally. I suppose—'

'Very funny,' Dora bit out caustically, putting her paint-pot and brush down on top of the ladder before starting her descent; with her luck she would have fallen halfway and ended up with *all* the paint on her, instead of just most of it!

'I realise this is a stupid question—'

'Then don't ask it,' she advised dryly, rubbing her sticky hands down her already paint-daubed denims. 'I would shake hands with you, but—'

'Shake hands, be damned!' He grasped her upper arms and pulled her towards him, kissing her hard on the mouth before releasing her again. 'After all, you were almost my sister-in-law,' he told her challengingly at the point where she would have protested, her face bright red with indig-nation.

Almost his sister-in-law did not give him the right to kiss her whenever he chose to do so! And she sincerely hoped, after that, that he wasn't even thinking about becoming engaged to someone else! 'As you can see, I'm busy, Griffin,' she told him pointedly.

He glanced up at the ceiling she'd been working on, and Dora's eyes reluctantly followed the direction of that mock-ing gaze. God, what a mess! Not only had she dripped most of the paint on herself, but the little she had managed to apply to the ceiling had dried in streaks, making it look dirtier than the original cream paint she had been trying to cover up!

'As I can see,' he murmured, the laughter clearly audible in his voice.

Dora glared at him. 'I suppose you could do better?' she

scorned—as far as she was aware, painting wasn't his forte, either!

His mouth twisted. 'I doubt I could do any worse,' he told her honestly. 'I'm just curious as to why you're doing it all? Surely finances aren't so bad that—'

'Finances have nothing to do with this,' she assured him sharply. 'Besides the shop premises themselves, my father left me quite comfortably off. No,' she continued firmly, having no intention of discussing her financial situation with Griffin, 'I was let down at the last minute by the shop-fitters. But, as the closure had been announced in all the local newspapers, and in the shop itself for several weeks, I decided to have a go at doing it myself.' The hot colour came back into her cheeks as she recalled the frustrating week she had just had.

The shopfitters she had hired to do this job hadn't let her know they wouldn't be able to do it until they had tele-phoned her at home on Sunday evening. And at such short notice she'd found it impossible to find a replacement; all of the other firms had told her the same thing; it was spring, their busy time, and they couldn't fit her job in for a number of weeks, if not months.

And so she had cleared the shop herself, carrying boxes and boxes of books out to the storeroom at the back of the shop. Once she had finally cleared it, and all the moveable furniture, she'd realised just how badly in need of repaint-ing the shop actually was. Her father had been content with the cream and brown, but for what she had in mind it wouldn't do at all. White and green paint was her colour scheme, with pine furnishings.

And so she'd been out and bought the paint she would need, and had embarked on doing the job herself.

The one thing she'd learnt was that it was nowhere near

as easy as it looked. Her respect for professional decorators had certainly gone up in the last few days!

'Need any help?'

She needed a *lot* of help—but not from Griffin! 'Thank you for the offer, but—'

'When, exactly, are you supposed to be re-opening?' Griffin cut in mildly.

Dora sighed heavily—trust Griffin to go straight for the jugular! 'I'll be fine, Griffin. With a little more practice I—'

'When, Izzy?' he prompted again. 'Because I'm pretty sure that no amount of "practice" on your part is going to make "perfect" in your case where painting is concerned!'

Two wings of colour burnt angrily in her cheeks. 'You really are the most insulting—'

'We've already covered that part of my personality,' Griffin dismissed derisively. 'Several times. Now tell me when, Izzy?'

'Ten days' time,' she admitted grudgingly. 'And I'm sure that if I carry on working—'

'Twenty-four hours a day for the next ten days—and it would still look a mess, Izzy,' he told her ruefully. 'I certainly couldn't do any worse!'

Her hands clenched frustratedly at her sides. It had been a terrible week, and she was doing the best that she could in the circumstances. She was going to hit him in a minute if he carried on tormenting her in this way—and she'd never been a violent person. She hadn't been a lot of things until she'd met Griffin Sinclair!

'It was nice of you to call in, Griffin,' she told him with dismissive politeness. 'But I'm sure I must be keeping you from something—or someone,' she added tartly, thinking specifically of Amanda Adams. 'So, if you'll excuse me—'

'Izzy, will you just, for once in your life, stop being so

damned independent?' He reached for her arm again. 'Accept an offer of help for exactly what it is. Even from me,' he added dryly.

He had made no comment, Dora noticed, on her remark about 'someone'... But she was sure Margaret wouldn't give up so easily. And Amanda herself hadn't seemed averse to the matchmaking...

She turned away. 'You're too busy—'

'Yes, I am,' he agreed ruefully. 'And I'm not saying I could come and help you during the day. But my evenings are free—and I'm quite happy to offer them to you for the next ten days!'

What about Amanda Adams...?

'Have you moved back to the house with your mother yet?' Dora asked pointedly; Margaret had made it more than obvious she would be most unhappy if Griffin spent all his spare time helping her.

He grinned. 'Why do you think I'm offering to come here and help you? Even painting is preferable to my mother's company! She's driving me nuts, Izzy; it's getting so desperate I've even thought seriously about offering to marry Amanda just for a quiet life. Except it wouldn't be,' he added grimly. 'Can you imagine it, with the two of them?'

Dora looked at him blankly for several seconds, and then she began to laugh. It was the first time she had even smiled during this last week. And inwardly she could acknowledge that one of the main reasons she had been so miserable was because she'd realised at the wedding that she was still attracted to Griffin, that she had actually been jealous of the attention he had shown Amanda Adams. The relief of hearing him making a joke about that situation was almost too much for her.

'I needed that,' she told him ruefully when the laughter finally stopped.

'I know,' he conceded gently. 'Do you have the makings of coffee somewhere in here?' He looked around at the chaos, at the dustsheets over the bigger pieces of furniture that Dora simply hadn't been able to move, not even an inch!

'It's a little soon for you to be expecting a coffee-break, Griffin,' she mocked dryly.

'It isn't for me,' he chided. 'You look as if you could do with a break. I'll make you a coffee: strong, hot and sweet. And while you're drinking it I'll see what I can salvage from the—um—'

'From the mess,' Dora finished for him ruefully, also looking about them. Not only had she got paint on herself, but it seemed to have splashed on to every other surface it could possibly reach, too. 'Mmm, coffee sounds a wonderful idea, Griffin,' she conceded wryly. 'But I'll make it; you salvage.'

Five minutes later two mugs of coffee were made, and Griffin returned from his 'salvaging'.

'Wrong paint, wrong brush,' he sighed, holding up the offending items. 'Either you were misinformed, or you didn't ask, and, knowing your independent nature—as I most assuredly do—'

'I'll go back tomorrow and get the right things,' she cut in firmly, knowing all too well what he was going to say about her independence.

But she had to be that way. There was no one else to ask for advice, not even her father now. Although she knew her father would never have agreed to the changes she was making!

'*We'll* go back tomorrow,' Griffin corrected pointedly. 'I like to know what I'm going to be working with!'

'Very well,' she conceded stiffly. 'But I thought you said you were working during the day?'

'Not on a Saturday.' He shook his head, taking a sip of his coffee. 'We'll make an early start tomorrow. It shouldn't take too long,' he looked about him thoughtfully. 'Now, have you eaten this evening?' He turned piercing green eyes on her.

She nodded.

'Such as?' he prompted dryly.

'Such as toast,' she answered defensively. 'About five-thirty. And I couldn't possibly—'

'—go out to eat looking like that,' he finished ruefully. 'No, I agree with you.' He smiled, having deliberately mis-understood her. 'We'll go back to your house, so that you can wash and change first, and then—'

'Griffin, even a wash and change of clothes isn't going to make me presentable enough to go out to eat in a res-taurant.' She pointedly touched the stickiness of her hair. 'Besides, I'm not hungry,' she told him stubbornly.

'Of course you are,' he dismissed crisply, looking at her critically. 'You're thinner than ever, Izzy,' he finally re-proved.

The loose fit of her clothes these last few weeks had told her that. But she wasn't used to being on her own yet, and cooking for one seemed such a waste of time and effort. Consequently she seemed to have subsisted mainly on toast and chocolate bars these last six weeks.

With the occasional glass of champagne—at Charlotte and Stuart's wedding—thrown in!

'Nonsense,' she dismissed brightly. 'You aren't very complimentary, Griffin.' Although, in the circumstances, her paint-daubed appearance included, that wasn't surpris-ing! But just once she would like him to think she looked—

'Izzy, you're beautiful—even covered in paint. I've always thought so. So don't fish.' He tapped her playfully on the nose.

Beautiful. That was what she had wanted him to think of her. But now that he had said it—

'And I haven't eaten yet,' he continued firmly. 'In fact I called in here on my way ho—back from the studio.' He grimaced at the mention of the house he wouldn't call home. 'The least you can do is keep me company.'

Dora raised auburn brows. 'And why should I want to do that?'

'It's best to keep the workers happy, Izzy.' He held out her jacket for her to put on. 'Especially the ones that are working for nothing!'

Dora took the jacket from him rather than put paint on that too. 'It won't be for nothing, Griffin,' she assured him determinedly, her gaze steady on his challenging one. 'The fitters I had hired were charging me a huge fee; I have no intention of letting you help me without—'

'Forget it, Izzy,' he rasped, turning her firmly in the direction of the door. 'You don't pay friends when they offer to help.'

He wasn't a 'friend'. She wasn't sure what he was. But they certainly didn't have that easy-flowing familiarity with each other that existed between friends. And that tenuous family link he'd claimed earlier was exactly that—tenuous! No, whatever it was she felt towards Griffin, it wasn't friendship...

'Take me out to dinner, Izzy,' Griffin put in before she could make any further objections. 'And we'll discuss my terms of employment!'

Dora couldn't say she particularly liked the sound of that, but she was quite happy to take him out to dinner. It would do for a start, anyway.

'Chinese okay?' she suggested lightly as she began to lock up. 'There's one quite near the house, and I can usually get a table at short notice.' Not that she'd been there for some time. Sometimes as a treat, when they'd been feeling tired after a hard day in the shop, she and her father would go and have a meal there together.

But she didn't seem to have been anywhere since her father had died. Except for the wedding, of course. She really would have to pick herself up once the shop was sorted out as she wanted it, and get out and about more.

'Fine.' Griffin followed her outside. 'We may as well take both cars and leave them at the house; I'm assuming we can walk to the restaurant?'

'We certainly can.' She nodded. After all that smell of paint, it was nice to be outside in the fresh air—even with the annoying and pushy Griffin for company!

She was glad of the separate cars on the way to her home. She hadn't felt able to draw a relaxed breath since Griffin's unexpected arrival. And strangely she felt much more confident about the decoration of the shop now that Griffin was going to lend her a hand...

Dora frowned at her own thoughts. Was it really sensible to let Griffin help her? With Griffin so determined, she wasn't going to have a lot of choice, she realised. And she had no doubt that he would do a much better job of it than she ever could—even with 'practice'!

But it would mean spending hours in his company... And she wasn't sure—

She looked up with a frown as the Jaguar, Griffin at the wheel, swept past her and took the lead. Typical of Griffin; he didn't like to take second place. Even, it seemed, when it came to driving the short distance back to her house.

But that wasn't what had made her frown. As Griffin had overtaken her in the Jaguar she'd realised, for the first time, that when he'd called to take her to the wedding last week he'd known how to find her home. She hadn't thought about it at the time—going to the wedding at all had been distressing enough!—but now it seemed slightly curious to her that Griffin had known where she lived without having to ask...

But that fact went completely out of her mind when she joined him outside the house a few minutes later.

'Now, you're sure there's no television, Izzy?' Griffin taunted as he stood beside her, waiting for her to unlock the front door. 'I would hate to have you proved—economical with the truth.' He grinned at her mockingly.

One of these days she was going to take great pleasure in wiping that smile right off his—

'I don't tell lies, Griffin.' She clearly stated the correct term for what he was implying, feeling very relieved when they were inside the house, as she found its elegant charm was always soothing to her nerves. Something Griffin certainly wasn't!

He quirked blond brows. 'Not even to yourself?' he murmured huskily.

'What would be the point of that?' Angry colour darkened her cheeks as she led the way into the sitting room.

He shrugged. 'None that I can see. But I'm told a lot of people do it.'

'Well, I don't,' she assured him firmly, preparing to leave the room. Without offering him a drink. He could damn well sit and stew for all she cared.

She knew that the reason she was so annoyed with him— this time!—was that he had touched on a sensitive nerve. She didn't exactly lie to herself about Griffin—she just didn't want to probe too deeply into what she felt for him!

'Need any help in the shower, Izzy?' he called after her softly.

Dora turned to give him a scathing glance. 'Save your charm for elderly ladies and star-struck teenagers, Griffin,' she snapped. 'It's wasted on me!'

He dropped down into one of the armchairs, part of a gold-coloured suite that was matched with antique oak furniture. 'Pity,' he drawled unconcernedly. 'No television,' he conceded ruefully after a brief look round the room.

She gave an irritated sigh. 'I told you I don't have one. But you're welcome to look through the books, if you'd like to.' She indicated the bookcase that dominated one wall of the room.

Griffin glanced across at the mainly leather-bound books. 'Your father's?'

She frowned. 'Mostly, yes.'

'Then I would rather not, thanks,' he rasped dismissively.

Dora shook her head, frowning again as she went slowly up the stairs.

All thought of Griffin's animosity towards her late father fled from her mind when she caught sight of her reflection in her bedroom mirror.

She looked a fright! Not only did she have paint in her hair and on her clothes, but spots of it all over her face too. No wonder Griffin had been so scathing about her ability to paint; it was a wonder she'd managed to get any on the ceiling at all when there was so much of it on herself!

Luckily the paint—even if it wasn't the right sort for the job—was washable, and fifteen minutes later, after her shower, she saw an altogether different reflection in her bedroom mirror. Her shoulder-length hair was brushed to a shining curtain of flame, while her black silk blouse and fitted black trousers complemented the slenderness of her figure—which wasn't too thin, no matter what Griffin might have implied to the contrary. The slight weight loss in her face emphasised her high cheekbones, giving a luminous appearance to the smoky grey of her eyes and a fullness to her curving mouth.

'Not exactly rags to riches.' Griffin stood up slowly as she entered the sitting-room. 'But I understand a little of what Prince Charming must have felt when he saw Cinderella!'

'I'll take that as a compliment,' Dora laughed softly, warmed by the admiration in his gaze.

'To make up for my earlier lack of one?'

He was standing too close again, Dora realised as she had trouble with her breathing once again. 'Having now seen myself—' she moved a safe distance away, to be able to breathe '—I realise the reason for that.' She laughed softly. 'Shall we go and eat?' she added brightly, suddenly finding the room claustrophobic. And Griffin, with his overpowering personality, was undoubtedly the reason for that.

He took a light hold of her arm as they walked to the door. 'It's the way to a man's heart, so I'm told,' he drawled.

'That's home cooking, Griffin,' Dora told him dryly, making no comment on his heart—although she was sure most women quickly learnt that he didn't have one!

Charles had once told her that Griffin had left a trail of broken hearts behind him ever since he'd reached puberty, and from his unattached state now, at thirty-four, he was probably still doing it. She certainly wasn't naïve enough to believe his charm!

'Charles reliably informed me that you are a more than capable cook,' Griffin taunted as they walked to the restaurant.

How strange that he should mention Charles, when she'd just been thinking of him herself. And 'a more than capable cook' sounded exactly like something Charles would have said.

Griffin gave her a sideways glance. 'Did you know that you frown like that every time my big brother's name is mentioned?'

'I do not!' Dora turned on him indignantly, frowning deeper than ever. 'In the circumstances, it would hardly be appropriate for me to burst out laughing,' she snapped. 'After all he is dead.' She drew in a deeply shocked breath, her eyes wide. 'I can't believe I just said that...' she groaned emotionally, shaking her head.

Griffin picked up one of her hands and tucked it snugly into the crook of his arm. 'As long as we both realise that it's an indisputable fact...' he murmured softly.

Dora gave him a sharp look, not at all happy with her hand being tucked into his arm like this. But the strength of his fingers as they rested on hers warned her she would have great difficulty in removing it.

'I'm hardly likely to forget it,' she bit out tautly.

Not that she wanted to forget Charles anyway, but with Griffin popping up in her life all the time, a constant reminder of the past, it was impossible for her to do that even if she wanted to. And move on...?

She felt a frisson of excitement and a certain amount of apprehension when she thought about her future. With no fiancé, and no father, she was completely alone for the first time in her life, with only the shop to direct her actions. And even her ideas for the changes there were a little frightening. If she should fail—

'Then it's about time you did,' Griffin rasped in answer to her last statement. 'Forget Charles, I mean,' he added grimly as she looked at him blankly.

In truth, in her quieter moments, when she thought of those brief months with Charles, she often had trouble remembering his handsome features, let alone what the two of them had talked about together. In fact, sometimes their engagement seemed as if it had happened to someone else.

But she wasn't about to tell Griffin that; he was far too familiar already, without that.

'Some of us don't want to forget him,' she told Griffin calmly. 'As you would appreciate—if you'd ever been in love yourself.'

She pitied Amanda Adams if Margaret ever succeeded in her plans for her and Griffin—because Griffin wasn't the settling down type. With any woman.

Griffin came to an abrupt halt, swinging her round to face him in the falling darkness. 'And just what makes you such an authority on my emotions, Izzy?' he rasped harshly. 'Sleeping Beauty still waiting for Prince Charming's wake-up call?' he added scathingly.

Dora's eyes glowed darkly grey. 'I thought you said I was Cinderella?' she bit out tautly.

'Same difference.' He shook his head disgustedly. 'They were both naïve!'

'Well, for your information—I'm not!' Dora glared at him. 'Neither am I asleep. Or a beauty. And as for Prince Charming—there is no such thing!'

'Have you ever tried looking beyond the end of your nose? Or are you—'

'*You're* beyond the end of my nose at this particular moment, Griffin,' she bit out scornfully. 'And no woman in her right mind would ever think of you in that— Oh!' She managed to gasp before Griffin's mouth came crashing down on hers.

It was a kiss without tenderness, and Dora felt the full force of Griffin's anger.

And then it suddenly changed, still not to tenderness, but to a searing passion that evoked a response from Dora. Her arms went up about his shoulders to stop herself from falling, and she felt as if she might snap in two with the steel band of his arms about her waist.

Finally Griffin pulled away. 'How's your sanity now, Izzy?' his eyes glittered down at her.

She swallowed hard, breathing shallowly. She had never seen Griffin like this before. She had seen him teasing, mocking, dismissively uncaring, but never moved by such anger that he looked ready to explode with emotion. She hadn't believed he was capable of such heated feelings; he always seemed to give the impression he was totally in control. Of any situation. But he was certainly very angry at this moment.

And Dora wasn't even sure why. What had been said, by either of them, that hadn't been said before, many times, to have caused such fury?

She was at a loss to even guess...

'Healthy enough to decide I don't want to have dinner with you, after all,' she answered firmly, able to imagine nothing worse than trying to have dinner with Griffin in this mood. The least she would end up with was indigestion. With Griffin in this unpredictable mood, she wasn't sure what the worst could be! Besides, she was more shaken by that kiss than she wanted him to even guess at! 'In fact,' she continued strongly, 'I think the whole idea of your helping me is a mistake. So perhaps it's best if we—'

'Chickening out again, Izzy?' Griffin cut in, his anger seeming to have faded as quickly as it had flared out of control.

Her eyes blazed at the taunt. 'I'm not "chickening out" of anything, Griffin,' she returned fiercely. 'You're rude, and arrogant, and I can do without your help!'

He stood back, his arms folded across the broadness of his chest. 'Now why the hell didn't you ever stand up to your father and Charles like this?' he murmured admiringly, with a humorous glint back in his eyes.

Dora blinked her surprise at that comment, becoming very still as its full meaning sank in. 'What...?'

'Because maybe if you had done so, even once,' Griffin continued huskily, 'you wouldn't have ended up as Dora the mouse.' He shook his head. 'Of course you wouldn't have been engaged to Charles, either, because he didn't want an Izzy, but that certainly wouldn't have been a bad thing!'

'What are you talking about?' Dora shook her head impatiently.

'I'm talking about the fact—Dora,' he added pointedly, 'that you let your father and Charles walk all over you, that you never once rebelled at the plans the two of them made for your future, that never once did you stand up and say what you wanted for your own life.'

'That isn't true!' Dora defended heatedly. Griffin made her sound like a doormat, not a mouse! 'My relationship with my father was my business,' she bit out angrily. 'As were the plans Charles and I had for our future together. And there's a perfectly good reason why I have no difficulty in arguing against *your* plans for me—'

'Yes?' Griffin prompted softly as she came to an abrupt halt in her dialogue.

She moistened dry lips. She would not back down; she must never back down where Griffin was concerned. Because he was more arrogant than her father or Charles had ever been, than the two of them put together!

'I loved my father and Charles,' she told him firmly.

'Yes?' Griffin prompted, more sharply this time, his eyes narrowed. 'Come on, Izzy,' he taunted as she hesitated. 'You may as well finish what you started!'

She straightened her shoulders, her gaze defiant now. 'Isn't it obvious, Griffin?' she scorned.

He shook his head. 'Not to me, no.'

She sighed her impatience. 'I find no difficulty in standing up to you because I don't love you!' she stated bluntly, not knowing *what* she felt for this man. 'Now, as I've already said, I've lost my appetite—' never more so than now! '—so if you will excuse me...' She turned and walked away, back in the direction of her home.

She knew Griffin would have to come back to the house some time this evening himself; after all, his car was there. But that didn't mean she would have to see him, she accepted with relief. He could just get in his car and drive away. For ever, as far as she was concerned! He was too disturbing, too—

'Er—Izzy...?'

She faltered in her step as Griffin called softly after her, stiffening her spine and bracing her shoulders before turning back to face him. 'Yes?' she prompted coldly.

'I'll call for you at ten o'clock in the morning,' he told her huskily. 'Make sure you're ready,' he added firmly as she would have spoken.

Part of her was so angry at him still that she wanted to tell him to go to hell, to tell him exactly what he could do with his offer of help. But the other half of her—

She didn't want to probe into what emotion controlled the rest of her feelings, she was becoming too frightened of what she might find there!

She did know that deep inside her she was relieved that he hadn't let her just walk away without speaking to her, and from what he'd said she knew that he still wanted to help her.

Besides, his offer of help was the only one she had!

And in ten days' time she had to re-open the shop, ready or not!

She was also, she realised with dismay, using excuses to explain away her relief that he had stopped her from leaving with this rift still between them...

'Ten o'clock.' She gave a stiff inclination of her head before turning on her heel and walking abruptly away. And this time Griffin didn't try to stop her.

Ten days. She could cope with seeing Griffin for ten days in a row.

Couldn't she...?

At this particular moment, with her senses still reeling from that kiss, she thought ten *minutes* would probably be too long!

CHAPTER SIX

'FOR God's sake, woman, will you hold the damned ladder steady?'

Dora drew in a sharp, controlling breath, biting her tongue to stop her angry retort, at the same time reaching out and steadying the ladder upon which Griffin stood.

The last five days of having him constantly about, issuing orders and expecting them to be carried out instantly, had been every bit as bad as she had thought they might be!

There was no doubting that Griffin was a hard worker, or that, surprisingly, he knew exactly what he was doing when it came to painting. In fact he had finished the painting last night, and was now on to measuring and fitting shelves.

Oh, yes, he was doing every bit as good a job as he had said he would. And yet...

'Maybe you're hoping I'll fall off the ladder and break my neck!'

She looked up guiltily at Griffin's mockery, only to look quickly away again when she found herself looking straight into laughing green eyes. She hadn't been wishing anything quite as drastic on him as breaking his neck—an ankle or an arm would do just as well!

This was awful! She had never had vengeful feelings like this towards anyone before. And yet Griffin—

'What are you making me for dinner this evening?'

And that was another thing! Although it was very kind of Griffin to help her in this way, she was not only seeing far too much of him than was even moderately comfortable, but he also expected her to feed him every evening once he had finished work for the day.

Good grief, it was almost as bad as being married to the man!

'What are *we* having for dinner this evening?' she corrected pointedly.

Because, as Griffin had pointed out oh-so-reasonably, she had to eat too, so they might as well eat their evening meal together. Waiting for Griffin to arrive in the evening, working together for several hours and then sitting down at her home to share a meal together implied an intimacy between the two of them that simply did not exist. In fact, Dora found it absolute torture, and her appetite seemed to desert her even before she sat down at the table opposite him.

'We have steak, Griffin,' she told him tightly. 'Which you are going to cook,' she added with satisfaction. 'I'm sure you can cook steak better than I can.' After all, he had to have lived on something when he'd been at home alone in his apartment.

He shrugged, coming down the ladder. 'Would this be because I mentioned—only mentioned, mind you—that I thought last night's chicken needed a little more white wine in the sauce?' He had reached the bottom of the ladder now, standing far to close to her.

So close, in fact, that Dora could feel the warmth emanating from his body...

She stepped back abruptly; even in paint-daubed clothes, old jeans ripped at the knees and a black tee shirt faded and worn, Griffin managed to look completely masculine and attractive.

And he hadn't just 'mentioned' last night that the sauce needed 'a little more white wine'—he had told her it was tasteless! But her father hadn't liked rich sauces and exotic meals; he had preferred plain English cooking, whereas

Griffin had told her on the first evening she'd made them a meal that the spicier his food was the better he liked it. At least she'd tried, hadn't she?

'Not at all,' she dismissed lightly. 'I simply thought I could concentrate on the salad and potatoes.'

Griffin grinned at her. 'Did you ever imagine the two of us would be cooking together?' he taunted.

Never, came the blunt answer.

After that one evening together at Dungelly Court, Dora had never imagined the two of them would ever meet again, let alone share the cooking of a meal in her home.

And, despite all the work Griffin was now doing for her, she couldn't help wishing they weren't about to do so now, either...

'I don't think of you at all, unless I absolutely have to,' she told him bluntly. And it was true; she didn't *dare* think about him!

He chuckled softly, shaking his head ruefully. 'Still no chance of my becoming egotistical in your company!'

'Did you think that might have changed?' she challenged tartly.

Griffin shrugged. 'One can live in hopes.'

'Not over that particular point,' she told him firmly. 'Now, do you still need me to hold the ladder for you, or can I get on with some things on my own?' She quirked an auburn eyebrow at him, a flush to her cheeks after this latest verbal exchange.

Griffin's expression softened as he looked at her. 'You know, Izzy, you really—' He broke off as the telephone began to ring. 'I know this is probably a silly question,' he murmured slowly as he looked about them speculatively, 'but where the hell is the telephone?'

Every surface was now covered with dustsheets after Dora's previous efforts with painting had ruined one bookcase where the dustsheet hadn't covered it sufficiently. And, like Griffin, Dora didn't have any idea where they had put the telephone, the desk where it usually sat having been removed completely from the room.

'I think we had better try to find it,' she muttered as the telephone continued to ring persistently, and started to lift the dustsheets to look beneath.

Griffin grimaced. 'Isn't seven-thirty a little late for a customer to be ringing?' He was looking under the dustsheets too now.

'How would I know? I'm not usually here at seven-thirty!' Dora came back impatiently, still looking for the ringing telephone.

'Good point,' Griffin conceded self-derisively. 'I— Aha,' he announced triumphantly as he pounced on the misplaced telephone. 'Classic Bookshop.' He spoke clearly into the receiver before Dora could get to it. 'Hello? Hello!' he said impatiently. 'Classic Bookshop,' he repeated more firmly. 'Look— Damn it,' he swore, looking accusingly at the receiver before replacing it back on its cradle. 'They hung up.' He scowled.

'It happens,' Dora dismissed, moving the telephone to where they would be able to locate it again more easily. 'Obviously a wrong number.'

Griffin frowned. 'Or someone who just didn't want to talk to me. I haven't messed things up for you, have I?' He looked at her with narrowed eyes. 'By answering the call?'

'I told you, it was probably just a wrong number.' Dora shrugged dismissively. 'Anyway, you were polite enough, so I can't see it being a problem—' She broke off abruptly as she realised what Griffin was asking her.

And the answer to his question was no. She had been out with Sam for a drink or a meal a few times, but certainly not on a regular basis, and there was no romantic relationship there, only companionship. So even if Sam had been the caller, there was certainly no reason why he should have abruptly ended the call when Griffin had answered instead of her.

Nevertheless, she could feel the embarrassed colour enter her cheeks as Griffin continued to look at her.

'So I *have* messed something up for you by answering the call,' he murmured slowly. 'I thought you told me there wasn't anyone in your life just now?' His eyes were narrowed accusingly.

Dora thought back to that conversation she had had with him over a month ago, when he had delivered her wedding invitation. 'As I remember it, I didn't actually answer that particular question,' she returned dryly. 'We were sidetracked into talking about my father's death,' she recalled heavily.

'So we were,' Griffin rasped. 'So who is he, this mystery man who hangs up the telephone when another man answers his call? More to the point—why isn't he the one here helping you with all this work?' He scowled darkly.

He was obviously far from pleased at the thought of her having a man in her life, Dora realised. Not that it was any of his business anyway, she thought resentfully; she could have a dozen men in her life if she felt inclined to do so! Well...maybe a dozen was a little excessive, she acknowledged ruefully, but just because she had been engaged to Griffin's brother, that didn't give him the right to make comments on her private life! She didn't dare even mention his!

She drew in a sharp breath. 'Who he is can be of no interest to you—'

'I think I would rather be the judge of that,' Griffin put in grimly.

'Where my private life is concerned, you have no right

to be the judge of anything,' she returned tautly, grey eyes flashing him a warning. Griffin had always been able to make her angrier than any other person she had ever met! 'I'm no longer a candidate for membership of the Sinclair family,' she dismissed, 'so, if you don't mind, I'll be the judge of my own friendships!' She was breathing hard in her agitation.

Griffin gave her a considering look. 'I saw this film once, where the female lead totally lost her temper with the hero; then he told her how beautiful she looked when she was angry, and before you knew what was happening the two of them ended up in bed together...'

Dora stared at him. What on earth was he babbling on about?

'I wouldn't even think about trying that with me,' she gasped, as the penny dropped. 'And I might remind you that you are the one who insisted on helping me out here—'

'Only because you were making such a damned mess of it on your own.' He scowled again. 'Where's this other man been for the last five days? Where is he now?'

She shrugged unconcernedly. 'Probably at the hospital. He's a doctor,' she explained, before Griffin could make any other assumption about her previous statement; he had a habit of twisting things and conversations to his own advantage!

'A doctor?' Griffin echoed disgustedly. 'You certainly know how to pick them, don't you, Izzy? One man dedicated to the advancement of his political career, and now this one, who's probably just as dedicated to medicine! Don't you think it would be nice to have a man dedicated to you for a change?' His eyes gleamed deeply green as he looked at her.

Her mouth twisted scornfully. 'That doesn't happen in this day and age—'

'Of course it does.' He snapped his impatience. 'It's just a question of finding the right man!'

'And just how can you be so sure that Sam isn't that man for me?'

'Sam—is that his name?' Griffin bit out hardly. 'Well, if Sam were the right man for you, Izzy, you wouldn't have spent most of Saturday and Sunday with me, or the last few evenings. Or is it a question of while the doctor is busy working at the hospital, the mouse is busy playing?' he grated disgustedly.

Dora gave a heavy sigh, shaking her head. 'I have no idea what you're talking about Griffin. Sam is a busy doctor, and we see each other when we can.' She had gone too far in this conversation now to explain the 'relationship' actually only consisted of three meals together, that, pleasant as Sam was, she certainly wasn't even close to being in love with him. Besides it really was none of Griffin's business; he didn't talk to her about Amanda Adams, either! 'And I'm not playing; this is damned hard work!'

'Tell me about it,' Griffin muttered. 'Hell, I can't believe— Why the hell didn't you tell— Oh, to hell with this!' He threw up his hands disgustedly before climbing back up the ladder, seeming unconcerned by the fact that it swayed precariously as he did so. 'A coffee would be nice, in about fifteen minutes,' he called down abruptly, before resuming his painting, pointedly ignoring her now, it seemed.

Yes, sir. Very good, sir. Three bags full, sir!

Dora was so angry at his peremptory tone that she was shaking with the emotion. What on earth was wrong with the man? Did he think that because she had once been engaged to his brother there should be no other men in her life?

No, she was sure he didn't think that... Hadn't he told

her weeks ago that in the same circumstances Charles would have replaced her long ago? Would probably be married to her replacement by now.

She looked up at him frustratedly, at his back firmly turned towards her as he continued the fixing of the shelf. She had thought of Griffin as an enigma when she'd first met him two years ago, but he was even more of one now. In fact, Dora didn't feel she understood him at all. His mood swings were completely unpredictable, as well as being, to her mind at least, illogical.

She hardly noticed the time passing, muttering to herself as she worked, and none of it complimentary to Griffin. She would be glad when the work here was finished and he disappeared again.

'It's one of the first signs, you know...'

Dora spun around at the sound of Griffin's voice so close to her ear, only to find him standing right next to her, a mocking smile curving those sculptured lips.

His bad humour of a short time ago certainly seemed to have disappeared—and transferred itself to her, Dora realised. 'What?' she snapped irritably.

'Talking to yourself.' He grinned unconcernedly in the face of her scowling expression. 'One of the first signs of insanity,' he explained.

'I'm not insane, Griffin,' she bit out impatiently, straightening away from him; he was far too close again. 'Mad, perhaps—but only angrily so. I suppose you want that cup of coffee now?'

He inclined his head. 'If it's not too much trouble...'

Dora gave him a scathing glance, putting her tape measure down where she would easily be able to find it again. 'When has causing trouble—in whatever form!—bothered you, Griffin?' she challenged. Trouble was his middle name!

He followed her through to the small kitchenette at the back of the shop. 'I—' He broke off as the telephone began to ring for the second time in half an hour. 'Want me to get that?' he drawled derisively, his gaze innocently wide.

She didn't even qualify his question with an answer, going back through the shop to answer the call. 'Classic Bookshop,' she recited impatiently, very conscious of Griffin as he stood in the doorway watching her.

'Dora?' Sam realised pleasantly. 'I haven't caught you at a bad time, have I? I did telephone the house first, but when there was no reply I remembered you'd mentioned having some work done at the shop...'

She caught a movement out of the corner of her eye, glancing up to find Griffin had moved further into the shop, that he was at this moment unashamedly listening to her end of the conversation as he leant against one of the larger bookcases, his arms folded casually in front of his chest.

'Sam!' she greeted him warmly. 'How nice to hear from you!'

'It has been a while,' he acknowledged ruefully, and Dora was easily able to visualise his pleasantly handsome face. 'But I realised you needed a little time to yourself after your father died. How are things?' he added gently.

'Fine.' At least they would be if it weren't for the infuriating Griffin!

'I wondered if you felt like coming out for a meal?' Sam suggested lightly. 'We could catch up on all our news.'

In Sam's case, unfortunately, that usually consisted of him talking endlessly of work and the hospital. But that had never really bothered her too much in the past; it had meant she wasn't required to do too much talking herself!

She glanced across at Griffin, turning quickly away again as he arched one eyebrow in enquiry. 'That sounds lovely, Sam,' she accepted lightly. 'When did you have in mind?

Tomorrow?' she repeated as he answered her, again glancing at Griffin. She saw he had now moved out into the middle of the shop, his hands held out pointedly at the half-decorated shop. 'Tomorrow would be lovely. Thank you, Sam,' she answered him firmly, determined not to be agitated by Griffin. 'I'll expect you about seven-thirty.' She rang off abruptly.

Griffin hadn't moved when she looked up again, his expression mildly scornful now. Dora gave him a questioning look.

He shrugged. 'I think you should have played a little harder to get,' he told her wryly.

She drew in an angry breath, that burning colour back in her cheeks. 'That isn't necessary where Sam is concerned,' she told him tartly, and meant it; Sam was at best a friend, and she knew that was all she was to him too. 'Is that how it's worked for you all these years?' she challenged Griffin. 'You've played so damned hard to get that every woman simply gave up in the end and went away!' she added scornfully.

To her annoyance, Griffin just smiled. 'Oh, I've allowed myself to get caught occasionally,' he murmured throatily. 'Very enjoyable it was, too.'

Dora's eyes flashed angrily. 'You're such a—' She broke off, breathing heavily in her agitation.

Part of the reason for her agitation, she realised, was the fact that Griffin could talk about that part of his life so casually. It was nothing to do with her, anyway. She should just feel grateful, after the temptation he had put before her two years ago, that she wasn't on his list of past conquests!

'Such a...?' he prompted, his softly green gaze unblinking.

Dora was the one to look away. 'A gentleman doesn't talk about past relationships,' she snapped.

Griffin laughed softly. 'Is that what Sam told you?'

She drew in a harsh breath. 'Hadn't we better try and get some more work done? After all, we won't be doing any tomorrow evening,' she added pointedly.

An evening away from Griffin's disturbing presence; it would be worth spending an evening in Sam's not-so-stimulating company just to escape Griffin for a few hours!

'And whose fault is that?' Griffin muttered as he moved the ladder and disappeared behind one of the heavy bookcases. 'So much for the urgency to get all this work finished in time.' He continued to complain, no longer in sight, his voice sounding slightly hollow. 'Sam calls and invites you out—and you just drop everything!'

'Not everything, Griffin, I can assure you' Dora contradicted dryly; she simply didn't feel that way about Sam.

'I suppose that's something,' Griffin muttered irritably.

Dora laughed softly, relaxing slightly. She couldn't help herself. Griffin sounded so disgusted by the whole thing. And, considering the bachelor life he'd enjoyed all these years, his attitude was more than a little hypocritical.

At least, it was the life he *had* led. No doubt living with his mother, and her marriage plans for him, had curbed all that!

'How are you enjoying living at home now, Griffin?' she called out, holding back a smile when all she could hear was his muttered expletives. 'Sorry?' she prompted with feigned innocence.

'I said,' Griffin bit out caustically, his voice still hollow as it came from behind the bookcase, 'enjoyment doesn't come into it! Even painting and building shelves here is preferable to going home,' he added disgustedly. 'My mother becomes more impossible to live with every day!'

'Nice to know I'm useful for something,' Dora called back tartly, inwardly wondering just how successful

Margaret had been so far in matchmaking Griffin with Amanda Adams. But Griffin never mentioned the other woman, and Dora was damned if she would ask him how things were going in that direction!

Griffin made no reply to this comment, and so Dora turned her attention to varnishing the rail a carpenter had installed yesterday. The rail cordoned off a section at the back of the shop that she intended turning into an area where customers could sit and browse through books while they enjoyed a cup of coffee. It was an idea she'd read about, from America, and it seemed to work very well, making choosing books more enjoyable for the customer.

It was just one of those changes she had told Griffin about. Another one was to increase the choice of books available. She simply didn't have her father's expertise when it came to classic books, and certainly wasn't qualified to restore them as he had done, and so she had decided, if she were to continue to run the shop at all, it had to be done her way. It was the only way.

Dora gave a puzzled frown as she heard the bell ring over the shop doorway as the door was opened, and then shut again. It was almost eight o'clock at night. Who on earth—?

She was glad Griffin was so close at hand, swallowing hard before looking apprehensively over the top of the railing she was working on.

Margaret!

Her apprehension didn't lessen in the least from knowing her unexpected caller wasn't a burglar, but Griffin's mother! She hadn't seen Margaret since the wedding, eleven days ago—but the memory of her last conversation with Margaret had stayed with Dora. As had the animosity the older woman had shown her.

What on earth was Margaret doing here, of all places?

More to the point, was Griffin, working behind the book-case, aware that his mother had just walked into the shop?

'Margaret,' she greeted in a loud voice, hoping to alert Griffin, wiping the varnish off her hands with a cloth as she did so. 'This is unexpected,' she understated, glancing nervously towards where Griffin was working undetected.

'Griffin has already left, I see.' Margaret wasted no time in niceties, having glanced around the shop and seen it was apparently deserted apart from Dora. Tall and slender in a black suit and cream blouse, Margaret gave Dora an icy look. 'I telephoned here earlier.' She answered the surprised look on Dora's face. 'I believe I am more than capable of recognising my own son's voice!'

Sam *hadn't* been that first caller. When the second telephone call had come, and it had been Sam, she had assumed, as had Griffin, that he had to have been the first caller too…

But it had been Margaret. And the reason she had rung off without identifying herself was that she had known it was Griffin who'd answered the call!

Griffin's car, like Dora's, was parked at the back of the shop, which was probably why Margaret hadn't seen it. And why the other woman had assumed—wrongly!—that Griffin was no longer here!

Dora moistened her dry lips. 'What can I do for you, Margaret?' she prompted warily; as far as Margaret was aware, there was no reason to be even remotely polite to Dora tonight…!

The older woman strolled further into the shop, looking about her critically before answering. 'I believe I have already expressed my—wish,' she bit out coldly, 'that you stay away from Griffin. A wish, judging by Griffin's presence here earlier this evening, that you seem to have totally ignored,' she added hardily, her eyes narrowed to steely slits.

Dora swallowed hard at the venom in the other woman's silkily soft voice, and glanced towards where Griffin was still hidden by the bookcase. Surely he must be able to hear this conversation...?

'As must already be obvious, Margaret, Griffin was the one visiting me. Not the other way round.' Dora kept her voice deliberately light—although part of her wanted to tell the other woman to just go away and leave her alone! Her father's death had been a shock, and Griffin's constant intrusion upon her life was far from relaxing; she wasn't sure how much more she could take without erupting. Griffin had likened her to a mouse several times, but at the moment that was the last thing she felt like!

Margaret's lips twisted disgustedly. 'Griffin always has had a soft spot for the injured and supposedly helpless,' she bit out insultingly.

'I am neither injured nor helpless!' Dora gasped indignantly. And she was becoming more than a little tired of this family's varying opinions of her.

Okay, so she was nowhere near as forceful as any of them, including Charlotte; nor did she find it necessary to step on people to get where she wanted to go, but that didn't make her the weak simpleton that Griffin, and now his mother, seemed to be accusing her of being!

'Aren't you?' Margaret drawled derisively. 'Then you play your part very well, my dear.'

'I—'

'Griffin is not for you, Dora,' the other woman told her, her eyes glittering furiously. 'Not now, or in the future, either. You—'

'How many times do I have to tell you that I don't want

Griffin?' Dora cut in heatedly, past caring that Griffin must be able to hear all this conversation.

If he wasn't prepared to reveal himself to his mother, Dora decided that it was his own fault if he heard no good of himself! His mother's intention seemed to be to link him with Amanda Adams, and at this moment, as far as Dora was concerned, the beautiful Amanda was welcome to him!

'Griffin broke a date with Amanda this evening so that he could be with you.' Margaret seemed to read at least some of her thoughts, her expression hardening even more.

He had...? But— 'Surely that is between Griffin and Amanda?' She met Margaret's gaze in defiance, even though she was slightly shaken at the fact that Griffin had preferred to come here and help her rather than be with the other woman.

Margaret shook her head disgustedly. 'Griffin has no idea what is or isn't good for him. And—'

'Oh, but he has.' Griffin had finally decided to break his listening silence. 'And, contrary to what you think, it certainly isn't Amanda Adams!' he added gratingly.

Margaret looked briefly stunned as Griffin could be heard descending the ladder behind the bookcase, collecting herself enough to shoot Dora an accusing glare as she realised her son hadn't already left after all.

At least, Griffin *began* to descend the ladder. But he only began—because seconds later there was a hoarse cry, and then a clatter, a thump, followed by a loud expletive.

By the time Dora and Margaret had rushed to his side behind the bookcase he'd managed to sit up, although he appeared to be having trouble getting to his feet.

'What on earth are you doing, Griffin?' his mother demanded, her scathing expression taking in his old, paint-daubed clothing.

The answer to that question had to be more than obvious, Dora would have thought!

Griffin sat awkwardly at the bottom of the ladder, a screwdriver—miraculously!—still held in his hand. The shelf he had been fixing had luckily remained in place, otherwise Griffin might have been more damaged than he appeared to be already!

Griffin looked up at his mother with glacial green eyes. 'Well, at the moment I appear to be sitting on the floor,' he snapped. 'But a few seconds ago I was standing at the top of this damned ladder listening to you warning Izzy to stay away from me!' If anything his expression seemed to become even colder at this last statement. 'Would you care to explain what the hell you thought you were doing?'

Dora looked at the older woman with a pained wince. Not that Margaret didn't deserve his anger, but Dora had never heard Griffin talk in that coldly menacing tone before, and was glad it wasn't directed at her. Although Margaret didn't look unduly perturbed by her son's obvious anger.

'It's obvious what I was doing, Griffin,' his mother scorned. 'For some reason you seem to have taken on some sort of responsibility for Dora since her father's death, and so I—'

'Hold it right there, Mother,' Griffin cut in angrily. 'I do not feel in the least responsible for Izzy. But even if I did, it would be none of your damned business!'

'Of course it's my business, Griffin,' his mother dismissed scathingly. 'You're my son—'

'To my regret,' he cut in harshly. 'But my being your son does not give you the right to choose my friends for me—especially at thirty-four years of age! Or—despite what you seem to think otherwise—the woman I marry,' he added forcefully.

'Amanda—'

'Izzy,' he corrected with a firm shake of his head, struggling awkwardly to his feet at last, although from the grey tinge that appeared in his cheeks at his did so the effort caused him more than a little pain. 'You seem determined that I marry someone, Mother, so, for the second time in your life—' he moved slightly, so that he could place his arm about Dora's shoulders '—I would like you to meet your future daughter-in-law—Isadora Baxter!'

Dora drew in a sharp breath, not sure who was the more shocked by his triumphant announcement—Margaret or herself!

CHAPTER SEVEN

'DORA?' His mother spat the name at him venomously. 'Are you out of your mind, Griffin?'

Margaret might have been the first of the two women to find her voice, but the words were the ones Dora would have spoken herself. She wasn't marrying Griffin!

And any guilty feelings she was having concerning her rather unsympathetic thoughts earlier about Griffin falling off the ladder were instantly nullified. If she'd had any idea at the time that he would make such a ridiculous statement only a short time later, she would have *pushed* him off the damned ladder!

'Not to my knowledge, no.' Griffin answered his mother dryly, standing awkwardly at Dora's side as he only seemed able to put weight on one side of his body. 'Izzy, I have no wish to be a nuisance, but I think…' He continued firmly as she would have told him just how much of a nuisance he was being! 'I think you should get me to the hospital as soon as possible,' he told her mildly. 'I may have broken my ankle.' He grimaced at the pain he was obviously feeling.

He did look very uncomfortable, she realised, somewhat guiltily. After all, she could vent her anger on him at any time, but if he was in enough pain to think he might have broken his ankle, perhaps she *should* get him to the hospital. She could kill him later!

'Can you walk?' she prompted concernedly.

'If you'll help me.' He nodded grimly. 'If you'll excuse us, Mother,' he added, his arm about Dora's shoulders as

127

she helped him to a chair while she got their coats and her handbag from the back room.

'Griffin!' His mother hadn't moved while they did this, her face a set mask, hands fisted tightly at her sides.

He glanced across at her coldly, seeming more comfortable now that he was sitting down, with the weight off his injured ankle, although there was still a white ring of pain about his lips. 'Are you still here?' he bit out caustically. 'I thought we had said all there was to say?'

To Dora's mind he'd said more than enough! And to Margaret's mind too, she was sure!

His mother's mouth tightened to a thin, angry line. 'Griffin, if you go through with this engagement—'

'It isn't a question of "going through" with it, Mother,' he drawled coldly. 'The engagement is already a fact.'

'If you go through with this engagement to Dora,' his mother continued determinedly, 'then I will totally wash my hands of you!'

He arched blond brows. 'Could I have that in writing?'

If anything Margaret's expression became more strained. 'I mean it, Griffin. This time there will be no eleventh-hour reconciliations—'

'Again, could I have that in writing?' he cut in scathingly. 'After the things you said earlier to Izzy, and the way in which you spoke to her, *you're* the one who should be apologising—and it isn't to me! But I know you too well to think you would ever do that,' he continued harshly as his mother looked set to make yet another threat. 'Let's just take it there will be one less guest to invite to the wedding, shall we?' he dismissed scornfully.

'Wedding!' Margaret's voice came out as a high-pitched screech. 'Griffin, I really can't allow—'

'I'm over twenty-one, Mother—*well* over! I'm not asking your permission, or indeed your approval, of the woman

I marry. Izzy…' He turned to her mildly. 'I really think I should go to the hospital now. My ankle is starting to swell up!'

'Swelling up' didn't adequately describe Griffin's ankle when Dora looked down at it—it was almost twice its normal size!

'Unless you want them to cut that boot off—' and although they were obviously old, they looked an expensive pair of boots '—I suggest we try and take it off now.' She bit her bottom lip worriedly, knowing the simple act of removing his boot was going to hurt him badly.

Not that he didn't deserve a little pain after making that ridiculous statement to his mother. She would just rather it wasn't from an injury he had sustained while working in her shop!

'Griffin, once I leave here this evening there will be no turning back,' his mother warned furiously as Dora knelt at his feet.

'Make sure you close the door on your way out.' Griffin didn't even bother to look up in order to answer her, too busy watching Dora as she slowly unlaced his bootlace. 'Just take it easy, Izzy,' he groaned, as if even the smallest amount of movement caused him severe pain.

She was doing her best, but every little movement seemed to hurt him. How was he going to fare on the drive to the hospital?

It seemed to take for ever to get the boot off his foot—a foot and ankle that seemed to be getting bigger by the second now that the constriction had been removed.

By the time Dora looked up from concentrating on this delicate task, it was to find herself once more alone in the shop with Griffin. Margaret had gone—and Dora hadn't even been aware of the bell ringing over the door as the other woman left!

Dora drew in a deep breath. 'Griffin—'

'Not now, Izzy,' he bit out between clenched teeth, his face even greyer than before.

Not now! He had just erroneously informed his mother that the two of them were engaged to be married, and he said 'not now'!

'If you don't get me professional help soon, Izzy, this may prove very embarrassing. For me, I mean,' he told her with a shaky sigh. 'I may just pass out!'

Dora needed no further urging on the need to get him to the hospital. There was no way she would be able to move him herself if he should collapse!

But as far as she was concerned this conversation was far from over. Griffin had to be told, had to be made aware that he couldn't go around making rash statements. Especially ones like the two of them were going to be married!

If the whole idea of it weren't so ridiculous it might actually be funny…!

'Slow down, Izzy,' Griffin grumbled from behind her. 'I haven't got the hang of these damned things yet!'

'These damned things' were the pair of crutches he had been issued with in the Accident and Emergency Department of the local hospital. After an examination, and X-rays, they had confirmed that he hadn't actually broken his ankle but badly sprained it.

Griffin had been enormously relieved that it wasn't broken—until the doctor had explained to him that a sprain was actually more uncomfortable than a break, and that it would probably take longer to heal. The doctor had also told him that he had to keep the weight off that ankle at least until the swelling and bruising abated, and that it could be several weeks in the case of the latter. Hence the crutches.

Dora turned to glare at him, the anger burning inside her giving her the extra impetus. 'How dare you name me as your next of kin?' she demanded furiously, having had great difficulty stopping herself from actually challenging his claim when they'd been in front of the doctor. Next of kin, indeed!

Griffin made his way awkwardly along the corridor to join her. 'Who else was I supposed to say?' he snapped impatiently. 'Charlotte is still on her honeymoon, and after that she's going to live in the States, anyway. And you heard my mother earlier—she's disowned me!' he reminded her grimly.

Because of his claim that he was engaged to Dora!

'She preceded me by only a very short time!' Dora assured him angrily. 'How dare you tell your mother the two of us are engaged to be married?' All the anger she had kept inside her suddenly broke free. 'I realise she's been pushing for you to marry Amanda Adams, but I object to being used to—' She broke off awkwardly as two nurses hurried past them in the busy corridor. Perhaps this wasn't the place to discuss this...

'Let's get out of here.' Griffin grimly shared her view, using the crutches to help him get along his injured ankle tightly bandaged for support. 'You can tell me how much you hate me once we're well away from here,' he added self-derisively.

Dora didn't hate him. She had never hated him. And she had realised just how much she didn't hate him when he'd made that announcement earlier to his mother about marrying her. It would be much better for Dora if she *did* hate him!

But she didn't… In fact, the opposite: she was in love with Griffin!

She had realised she was still attracted to him at Charlotte's wedding; she just hadn't realised how much. Just for a moment, a brief, yearning moment, tonight, after he'd announced their engagement to his mother, she had *ached* for it to be true…!

She had been attracted to him at Dungelly Court two years ago; of course she had. She'd thought of him often in the weeks that had followed her return home, and had longed to see him again, to see the laughter in those deep green eyes, to know the warmth of his arms about her once again.

But Griffin knew her name, she'd reasoned, also knew the area she lived in with her father, knew that she helped him run his bookshop. So if Griffin had wanted to see her again she wouldn't have been that difficult to find. But Griffin obviously *hadn't* wanted to find her. He must have thought of their encounter as no more than that—if he'd thought of it at all!

And so Dora had done her best to forget about him. She'd made no connection at all between her local political candidate, Charles Sinclair, and the man she had met in Devon. Why should she have done? The two men had been complete opposites—to look at, as well as in their manner. Besides, Griffin had kept to himself the fact that his own family lived in the neighbouring country of Berkshire. In fact, when she thought back to those few brief hours of knowing him, he had told her very little about himself at all.

Her father had been a leading helper in Charles's political campaign, and when he'd introduced the two of them it had seemed perfectly natural to Dora to accept Charles's invitation, when it came, for her to go out to dinner with him.

The following months as Charles's social partner had been busy ones, so much so that she had managed to put Griffin into a locked compartment at the back of her mind. And heart.

Until he had been introduced to her, six months later, as Charles's younger brother!

But when, exactly, had she fallen in love with Griffin?

Dora glanced at him now from beneath lowered lashes as they made their way slowly to the car park. Did it really matter when it had happened? She was in love with Griffin now, and knew herself to have been so for some time.

She loved Griffin!

And he was a man no woman in a completely sane frame of mind should possibly fall in love with...!

'Get in,' she rasped, after unlocking her car, glancing across the roof of the vehicle at him impatiently as he made no effort to do so. 'Griffin, it's late, and—'

'And you haven't eaten,' he acknowledged dryly. 'I've noticed you get—irritable, if you aren't fed properly,' he explained ruefully at her blank look.

'My—irritability, has nothing to do with my not having eaten yet this evening!' she assured him tartly. 'If you would just get in the car—'

'That's just it—I can't,' he admitted softly. 'Sorry, Izzy.' He grimaced at her frowning expression. 'But I can't manage the crutches and get into the car at the same time!'

Dora moved around the car to stand at his side. The car door stood open. Griffin had obviously managed to do that, but that was as far as he had got. The act of putting aside the crutches and levering himself into the car was obviously just too much for him.

This sprained ankle, Dora realised with an inward groan,

was going to be a damned nuisance. Along with Griffin himself!

She sighed. 'Give me the crutches while you hold on to the roof of the car and swing yourself inside,' she decided with a frown.

To give Griffin his due, he only lost his balance once during this negotiation, instinctively putting his injured foot to the ground, instantly giving a pained groan, his skin taking on the sickly pallor it had in the shop earlier. Although, again to give him credit, he carried on with the manoeuvre, finally settling himself down into the passenger seat, his injured foot slightly elevated.

'As my mother has thrown me out, we may as well go back to your place,' he muttered grimly, his head resting back wearily against the seat, his eyes closed.

He looked terrible, Dora acknowledged. And having to ask for help couldn't be easy for a man like Griffin.

No! It was bad enough that she had realised she loved him; the last thing she needed was to start feeling sorry for him, too.

Although he *had* injured himself while helping her out at her shop...

She was doing it again!

None of this excused the outrage he had committed earlier. She hadn't exactly been thrilled herself by the things Margaret had said to her, but it would never have occurred to her to retaliate in the way that Griffin had. And she had no doubt that Margaret meant every word she had said; she wasn't going to forgive Griffin easily for announcing his intention of marrying Dora. If, indeed, Griffin ever asked for forgiveness...

Dora glanced irritably at Griffin, only to find that he seemed to have fallen asleep. With his eyelids closed over those mocking green eyes, all cynicism wiped from his expression, Griffin looked somehow younger, and—and vulnerable. And that was something she had never associated with Griffin, of all people. He would look like this when he was asleep in bed. But then his chest would be bare, the golden hair—

Acknowledging—to herself, at least—that she loved Griffin was one thing; having erotic fantasies about him was something else entirely!

Besides, any fantasies she might have about him would be instantly dispelled the moment he raised those sleepy lids and opened his mouth to tease her about her feelings. Because Griffin might kiss her occasionally, and seem to enjoy it, but he enjoyed teasing and tormenting her more than he did kissing her.

'What are you thinking about?'

She hadn't been aware that Griffin had woken beside her— There she went again; they were in a car, for goodness' sake, not in bed together!

Griffin was still sitting relaxed against the car seat, but his head was now turned in her direction, that steady green gaze fixed on her questioningly.

Dora turned hastily away again, unnerved after her own intimate thoughts.

'You looked—wistful,' Griffin murmured curiously.

Wistful! Was that how she looked when plagued with a physical need for this man? Plagued—because she couldn't think how else to describe these feelings she still had towards Griffin. They certainly weren't welcome feelings!

And neither was Griffin himself, as they reached her home. They had dined here together the last few evenings, and each time they had Dora had been made aware of the fact that her father would never have invited Griffin here, that Griffin was out of place in the mahogany-furnished dining room and the austere sitting room.

He looked no less so this evening as Dora helped him in from the car and on to the leather sofa, his injured leg stretched across the other two cushions.

Dora straightened abruptly. 'I'll go and get us both some dinner; I'm sure you must be feeling hungry yourself by now.' Although she had lost her own appetite since realising her feelings towards this man...

Griffin's mouth twisted ruefully. 'I thought I was cooking the steaks this evening,' he reminded her.

Dora smiled, shaking her head as she straightened. 'I'll manage. I'll come through and get you once the food is ready.'

He gave a self-disgusted sigh. 'Finally got me where you want me, hmm?' he ground out harshly.

She gave him a sharp, defensive look. Had he somehow guessed she was in love with him? Had she been so shaken herself by the discovery that she had given herself away?

'At your mercy!' He grimaced his own disgust at that fact.

She *hadn't* given herself away, Dora realised with relief.

So relieved was she that she gave him an impish grin. 'It's certainly a novel experience!' she conceded, still smiling.

His gaze narrowed. 'Don't get used to it, Izzy,' he warned her softly. 'I may not be as mobile as I would like to be, but I can still talk!'

Her smile faded. 'I think you've talked quite enough for one day, don't you?' she reminded him.

Now it was Griffin's turn to smile. 'I think it's as well that I left most of my stuff at my apartment in town rather than taking it to Mother's house—including those replacement books you got for me,' he recalled ruefully. 'Otherwise my mother would no doubt enjoy disposing of them all over again!'

Griffin had done as she'd asked and given her a list of the books his mother had destroyed. And, apart from two that were completely out of print, Dora had managed to get him replacement copies for his own collection.

Dora was glad he found this situation so amusing; she didn't find it in the least funny!

'No doubt,' she conceded dryly. 'Do you think Margaret is really serious about disowning you?' But even as she asked the question she knew the other woman was deadly serious; Margaret was not a woman who allowed herself to be thwarted without due retribution. Griffin had upset all her plans for herself, as well as for him; Margaret would never forgive him.

Griffin grinned unconcernedly. 'Does it matter?'

Dora frowned. 'I thought the two of you had come to some sort of agreement because of Charlotte's wedding?' In the same way as she had promised Charlotte she would keep an eye on Griffin—she just hadn't expected it would be this close an eye...

'We did,' he acknowledged dryly. 'But the agreement was for me to spend six months living at the house with my mother—not that she could pick out a wife for me!' His eyes had become glacial as he talked of his mother. 'And Amanda Adams is not for me. No matter what my mother may have planned to the contrary,' he added grimly.

Dora shrugged as unconcernedly at she could at the mention of the other woman. 'You obviously thought her attractive enough to invite her out to dinner this evening.' And with her own newly discovered feelings towards Griffin that fact didn't please her one little bit! The other woman was far too beautiful.

'Actually,' Griffin drawled softly, 'Amanda was the one to do the asking—but it would be extremely ungentlemanly of me to reveal that!'

Dora gave him a scathing glance. 'Extremely!' she agreed. Amanda had asked Griffin out? She knew she could never have been that bold herself. But then, the other woman had obviously been aware of Margaret's intentions towards Griffin and herself—and must have been agreeable to them.

He shrugged. 'I've never claimed to be a gentleman. Besides, I've never liked scheming women, either.' His eyes had narrowed grimly. 'And it seems to me that Amanda was in collusion with my mother over this. One of them is bad enough, but heaven help any man who has two scheming women in his life! Besides, Izzy,' he added softly, 'I think you missed the whole point of my mother's remark; I broke that dinner engagement with Amanda so that I could come to the shop and help you.'

Fixing shelves was preferable to him than having dinner with the beautiful Amanda? Or dared she read more into that than Griffin had actually said? That he preferred spending time with her rather than Amanda...?

No, she didn't dare!

Griffin was one of the most unpredictable men she had ever known; it would be a mistake to read anything into his actions!

'As you sprained your ankle in the process,' she reminded him derisively, 'you may have been safer keeping your date with Amanda!' That was her parting shot before escaping to the kitchen to prepare their meal.

Escaping because it was the first time she had been alone to collect her thoughts since she had realised how she felt about Griffin!

She leant weakly back against one of the kitchen units. What was she going to do about loving Griffin? What could she do?

Nothing, came the blunt answer to her question. If Griffin

had been going to feel anything towards her—other than amusement!—then he would do so by now.

What he *did* feel towards her, she was slowly realising, after Margaret's earlier comment, and although he might deny it, was a certain sense of responsibility. And that was probably because of her engagement to his brother, and now that she had been left alone in the world after her father's death. How had Margaret put it? 'Griffin has always had a soft spot for the injured and supposedly helpless'!

Pity. That was what that amounted to. And she didn't want Griffin's pity.

The mere idea of it filled her with a restless anger, and as she banged about in the kitchen preparing their meal she was barely aware of what she was doing, all the time muttering to herself. Pity, indeed! She was twenty-six years old, with no ties and enough money that she shouldn't have to ever worry about it; Griffin could damn well keep his pity! Maybe she would get help in the shop, travel a little herself, maybe even think about that university course she had once wanted to do.

'What have those steaks ever done to you?' mocked an amused voice.

Griffin, of course. Dora spun round to find him standing in the doorway, leaning against the doorjamb, obviously having made his way here on his crutches. Dora had been making so much noise herself that she certainly hadn't heard his approach. How long had he been standing there watching her? More to the point, had he heard any of here mutterings?

Griffin raised mocking brows. 'You're slamming that poor defenceless steak around as if you wished it were—me!'

Not him, exactly, she inwardly conceded, just these un-wanted feelings she had found she had for him.

Not that she felt she was to blame for feeling about him the way she did. As that elderly lady had pointed out in the shop weeks ago, Griffin was an extremely attractive man. He could be warm and kind too, and was inevitably laughing at something, quite often himself. It was just that he was the complete opposite of her; her own nature was quiet, and a little reserved—and she certainly had no illusions about herself attracting a man as handsome and popular as Griffin was.

So he had guessed right; she was angry, but not at him, at herself, for having been so foolish as to fall in love with him...

'Not at all.' She gave a rueful grimace, not quite able to meet his teasing gaze, feeling suddenly shy. 'I was just told that it's best to tenderise the steak while cooking it,' she excused awkwardly.

Griffin grinned. 'I don't think battering it into submission qualifies!'

The steaks were ready now, thank goodness, putting an end to any further remarks about her treatment of the meat.

Within five minutes Dora had the plates on the table, and had helped Griffin into a chair. Not that he looked very comfortable once he was seated.

'Would you be better on the sofa with a tray?' she offered, as each movement seemed to cause him pain.

'I would be better if I had never fallen off the damned ladder,' he rasped impatiently.

'Eavesdroppers never hear any good of themselves,' she quoted ruefully. 'Or attain a good impression of the people doing the talking!' Not that she thought his opinion of his mother had been that high in the first place, but he couldn't have any illusions left after what he had overheard earlier.

'You should have made your presence known much earlier than you did.'

'And missed hearing my mother in full flow?' he scorned with a grimace. 'She obviously had plans for me, both privately and professionally. Plans I want no part of. So, it looks as if you're stuck with me,' he shrugged.

Dora swallowed hard, feeling the colour leave her cheeks. 'I'm aware you were hitting out at your mother when you announced your engagement to me. I don't intend holding you to it—'

'I think you've already made your feelings about that more than plain,' Griffin drawled self-derisively. 'You would as soon be struck down with the plague as marry me!'

That wasn't exactly true. It was only if he married her just to spite his mother. She would rather contract *any* deadly disease than go through with that. And on Griffin's side there would never be any other reason for going through with such a ridiculous plan...!

'I wasn't actually referring to that particular "stuck with me",' Griffin continued dryly, at her lack of response to his earlier comment. 'As you can see, I'm pretty incapacitated at the moment, and the doctor said that I'll probably continue to be so for several more weeks. My apartment in town is your typical bachelor home—no food stocked in for an emergency, no one to help with the cooking and cleaning. And now that my mother has thrown me out, I have nowhere else to go...'

Dora had a terrible feeling she knew exactly what this was leading to. And she didn't like it one bit!

'Not that I'm willing to go back there, anyway,' he added grimly. '"No eleventh-hour reconciliation"!' He disgustedly repeated his mother's earlier warning. 'I only went back there this time for Charlotte's sake. My mother will be the one who does the apologising this time—to both of us!' he announced firmly.

And as Dora could never see that happening—to Griffin, let alone to her—mother and son were destined to remain estranged...

But Griffin was straying away from the point. 'You were saying...?' Dora prompted faintly, her lips feeling stiff and unyielding. In fact, all of her felt stiff and unyielding, as if she were suddenly carved out of stone.

'I was saying, Izzy...' Griffin gave her that endearing grin '...that by "stuck with me" I meant that I have nowhere else to go. I can't drive. I can barely walk, damn it. So, if it's okay with you, I'll just stay here for a week or two, until I'm back on my feet.'

But she did mind! It was impossible. He couldn't stay here, in close proximity to her, night as well as day.

He just couldn't!

She just couldn't...!

CHAPTER EIGHT

'IT's the guest bedroom,' Dora told Griffin stiffly an hour or so later as she showed him into the room.

They had finally eaten—at least, Griffin had eaten; Dora's appetite seemed to have deserted her once she'd realised she might be 'stuck with him' for some time. Over that hour she had looked at this particular problem from every angle she could think of—and at the end of it Griffin's solution that he stay there with her seemed to be the only viable one. Griffin had already pointed out the drawbacks to going to his own apartment, and apologising to his mother and admitting he had lied about his engagement to Dora didn't even seem to be an option. A hotel didn't seem the answer, either. Food and clothing wouldn't be a problem for him there, but he would still have the fact that he wasn't particularly mobile to contend with.

No, she had concede heavily a short time ago, much as she disliked the idea of Griffin staying here with her, there was nowhere else he could go. Besides, she had an obligation to him, didn't she? He had been injured while working in her shop.

'It's great,' Griffin enthused, at what was actually only a room that had the bare essentials: carpets, curtains, a wardrobe and dressing table and a bed. Although he seemed to find the latter comfortable enough when he dropped down on to it, the effort of coming up the stairs obviously having proved more tiring than he cared to admit.

Dora and her father hadn't had many guests come to stay, and so this third bedroom, while being clean and bright, was actually quite characterless. She decided she could brighten it up a little tomorrow, with some flowers and possibly a few ornaments, but for the moment it would just have to do.

'The bathroom is opposite,' she told Griffin distantly. 'The room next door on this side was my father's. I haven't found the time to—clean it up yet.' She couldn't quite meet Griffin's gaze as she made the last comment.

It had nothing to do with finding the time to clean out her father's room; it was really due to a reluctance on her part to do so. Her father had been a very private man, and apart from changing the bedlinen and vacuuming and dusting once a week Dora had never gone into his bedroom when he was alive. It somehow seemed even less right to do so now that he was dead. Although she knew she would have to do it one day. Just not yet...

'My father's bedroom is bigger than this, of course,' she began slowly.

'I'll be just fine in here, thank you, Izzy.' Griffin squeezed her arm understandingly. 'And you seem to have missed something out of your verbal tour of upstairs...'

'I did?' Dora turned to him, frowning. She had told him where the bathroom was, made it more than obvious she would rather he didn't wander into her father's room; what else could she possibly—? Her cheeks burned fiery red as the answer to that question hit her. 'My bedroom is the door at the end of the hallway,' she told him awkwardly.

Griffin chuckled softly at her obvious embarrassment. 'I know this is probably a unique experience for you, Izzy, having a man upstairs in your home who isn't your father, but—'

'And just what makes you assume it's unique?' Dora was stung into retaliating. 'I'm twenty-six years old, Griffin, and I haven't taken vows of chastity!' Although just that old-

fashioned description of virginity reminded her all too forc-
ibly of their initial meeting at Dungelly Court, when for a
brief time she had been completely 'Izzy'!

This situation, the two of them alone here in her home,
was altogether too seductive—

'And would the man in question have been my brother
Charles, or the current Sam?' Griffin's scorn cut in on her
panicked thoughts.

She no longer felt panic—just anger, her eyes sparkling
deeply grey as she glared at him. 'I don't think that's any
of your business—do you?' she challenged.

His mouth was a grim line. 'If it was Charles, then, yes,
I think it might be my business,' he bit out harshly. 'You—'

'Well, I don't,' Dora told him grimly. 'This engagement
isn't a real one, only a figment of your mother's imagination, so you have no need to worry about my reputation,'
she added disgustedly. 'And, let's face it, Griffin, if we
really were in a romantic position, where we felt it necessary to make confessions about past relationships, I would
be here all night listening to yours!' she scorned derisively.

Griffin looked at her wordlessly for several seconds before seeming to visibly force himself to relax. 'You might
be surprised,' he finally murmured dryly.

'Surprise is probably the least of what I would feel!'
Dora dismissed, taking some extra towels out of the wardrobe. 'I'll leave you to get settled in.' She put the clean
towels on the bed before walking to the door. 'I still have
to clear away downstairs.'

And she made almost as much noise clearing away from
dinner as she had when preparing it! Who the hell did
Griffin think he was? He had no right to question her relationship with Charles, and as for Sam—they simply didn't
have a romantic relationship.

Sam...!

He was meant to be calling for her here tomorrow evening at seven-thirty!

She sat down heavily on one of the kitchen stools. Twenty-four hours ago her life had been calm and uncomplicated—boring, even, she inwardly acknowledged. The house had been feeling so empty since she'd been living here on her own. Now she not only had a male house guest—for an indefinite period!—but she also had a date tomorrow evening with another man. A man who was calling at the house for her. And Griffin, being Griffin, would make sure he was well in evidence when that happened!

Uncomplicated! She felt as if her life had been violated, taken over. And, loving Griffin as she did, she couldn't see any end to the torment...

'Wakey, wakey, Izzy. Rise and shine! And it is shine too; it's a beautiful day outside.' The bedroom curtains were thrown back to accompany this last announcement, that bright sunshine at once illuminating the bedroom.

And blinding Dora where she lay groggily back against the pillows in her bed.

Griffin!

Not only had he invaded her bedroom at goodness knows what ungodly hour, but he was cheerful doing it!

Dora was not a morning person. When her father was alive the two of them had barely spoken to each other in the mornings, both knowing what needed to be done and getting on with it. And that regime had continued quite smoothly for Dora since she had been on her own.

Not any more, apparently!

'This is amazing.' Griffin continued talking at her lack of a response. 'You must have hundreds of unicorns in here!'

Her collection of unicorns! And Griffin was right; there

were hundreds of them. She had been collecting them since she was a little girl, an indulgence her mother had approved of—although it had been tacitly agreed between them from the beginning that these beautiful mythical beasts would remain in her bedroom, where her father wouldn't have to be bothered by them. And so no one other than her mother and herself—despite what she might have said to Griffin the evening before, concerning having men upstairs in the house—had ever seen her collection of unicorns. Until Griffin...

And she wished he hadn't seen them, either. These unicorns, mythical and beautiful, were an indication that Dora Baxter wasn't as no-nonsense and practical as she liked to appear to be. The very last thing she wanted Griffin, of all people, to know!

The sooner she diverted his attention away from the existence of the unicorns, the better!

She rolled over with a protesting groan, taking the sheet with her, looking up at Griffin through half-closed lids, the light still too bright for her to focus properly.

He had obviously been up some time, was dressed and freshly shaved by the look of his healthily glowing face. But he didn't have any toiletries with him, least of all a razor...

'My razor isn't meant for a man's stubble,' she told him in a disgruntled voice, realising that must have been what he had used for his shave.

'And a good morning to you too!' Griffin grinned good-naturedly as he dropped down on the end of her bed. 'Has anyone ever told you how beautiful you look in the morning?' he added teasingly.

Dora looked at him warily. 'Is this a trick question...?'

'Not at all,' he dismissed lightly. 'I was merely going to tell you they were lying if they had!' He grinned again.

Dora looked up at him through jaundiced eyes. 'Has anyone ever told you what a pain it is to be woken by someone as cheerful as you in the morning?' She struggled to sit up, which wasn't easy with Griffin sitting on the bedclothes, especially as she had every intention of keeping the sheet in front of her for protection. 'What time is it?' She couldn't focus on her bedside clock yet, her eyes still gritty from lack of sleep.

'Seven-thirty,' he told her unconcernedly, shaking his head mockingly as she groaned at the earliness of the hour. 'I never figured you for a late sleeper, Izzy!'

'Then you figured wrong, didn't you?' she snapped irritably, pushing back the auburn curtain of her hair. 'Any time before eight o'clock in the morning and I consider it to still be night. It's only on special occasions—'

'And my being here isn't special?' Griffin put in tauntingly.

'Your being here is many things, Griffin,' she sighed, giving him a scathing glance, 'but special isn't one of them! I was referring to birthdays and Christmas.' Although it didn't surprise her in the least that Griffin was an early riser; he was hyperactive most of the time! 'Where's the coffee?' She yawned tiredly.

He grinned at her again. 'You may not be beautiful in the morning, Izzy,' he chuckled. 'But you're certainly good entertainment value!'

'Thanks,' she dismissed uninterestedly. 'Now where's the coffee?'

'I can't get down the stairs without help—remember?—let alone get back up again with a cup of coffee in my hand.' He stood up with the help of his crutches. 'Otherwise I would willingly have brought you coffee in bed.' *And joined you there*, his expression seemed to imply.

Dora was much more awake now, and the more fully

awake she became, the less she liked Griffin's presence in the sanctuary of her bedroom. Beautiful or not, the two of them were still alone here, and Griffin was irrepressible—in every way!

'If you would like to wait outside for me, I'll get dressed and make my own coffee.' As she did every other morning. 'And then you can explain exactly why it is you've woken me up this early,' she added warningly.

'I'll do that.' Griffin nodded mockingly, making his way awkwardly to the door.

There was much more to this cohabiting than she had realised, Dora decided disgruntedly as she washed and dressed. She had never lived away from home, had no experience of having to live with anyone other than her immediate family, and they had always been in tune with each other enough to respect the other's space. Griffin didn't even seem to realise she needed space, let alone respect the fact!

As if to confirm that, she almost fell over him as she came out of her bedroom, finding him leaning against the wall directly outside.

The withering look she gave him would have been enough to silence any other man, but not the unstoppable Griffin.

'The butterfly emerges,' he drawled with barely suppressed humour as he straightened in preparation for following her down the stairs.

Dora decided then and there that she wasn't even going to speak to him again until she had prepared and drunk her first cup of coffee. A few days ago she had found the house lonely and empty—now she found it much too full!

'Now…' She sighed her satisfaction a few minutes later, taking a sip of the rich coffee she had made for them both, Griffin having sat and watched her every movement with unconcealed humour. 'What could possibly be so urgent you had to wake me at this ridiculous hour?' she asked.

He bit his lip to stop himself from grinning once again. 'You really weren't joking about that, were you?'

She raised auburn brows. 'What on earth made you think that I was?'

'Never mind.' He shook his head. 'I woke you at this "ridiculous hour" because we have to go to my apartment so I can pick up a few things, and then you have to drive me to the studio. I'm filming at the moment, remember?' he reminded her as she looked blank.

He had told her he was, yes, which was the reason he could only help her at the shop in the evenings. But surely with his badly sprained ankle...?

'Won't you have to delay that for a while?' She frowned.

'You obviously aren't familiar with television studios, Izzy. Or television companies, come to that,' he drawled. 'They don't wait for time or tide, let alone any man!'

Dora still frowned. 'But surely the programme revolves around you?'

'Exactly.' He nodded. 'And I can't let a little thing like a sprained ankle delay filming.'

'But—'

'The minutes are ticking away, Izzy,' he warned, standing up after finishing his own coffee. 'And we do have to go to my apartment first. I need to change and pick up some things—like clothes and a razor,' he added pointedly.

Dora had no wish to go to his apartment, let alone drive him to the studio for filming. She had become too embroiled in his life already, and had no wish to become any more involved. Loving him as she did, her life was going to be empty enough after he left without that!

'Can't the studio send a car for you?' She voiced her own reluctance to make the drive. 'With you unable to help out at the shop any more I have some things of my own I need to sort out today.' Like finding someone to finish the rest of the work!

'No, they can't send a car for me, Izzy,' Griffin bit out with controlled impatience. 'I don't ask for superstar status, and they don't offer it. Besides, have you forgotten I sustained my injury while—?'

'—helping me,' Dora finished wearily. 'We've been through that one already, Griffin,' she sighed. 'I accept responsibility—I just don't expect it to last for ever!'

He looked at her wordlessly for several seconds, and then he relaxed. 'You really are crabby in the mornings, aren't you?' He sounded amused again.

More so this morning than usual, she inwardly acknowledged. And with due reason. She had lain awake for hours last night after going to bed, unable to sleep for thinking of Griffin in the house with her. In fact, when he had woken her, half an hour ago, it had felt as if she had only just gone to sleep!

'I am.' She nodded, not even attempting to defend herself, getting up to rinse their coffee cups. 'I'll just get my jacket and bag.' And her shattered equilibrium, she hoped!

Snap out of it, Dora, she told herself as she went to collect her things. If she carried on behaving like this Griffin would guess something was wrong, that something inside her had changed. And if he should ever guess it was because she was in love with him, she would never be able to face him again!

'Now, isn't this cosy?' Griffin turned to grin at her once they were in the car and on their way. 'It's almost domesticated.'

She gave a rueful smile. 'I can't ever imagine you as domesticated!'

'Can't you?' He sobered. 'But I can assure you, I'm completely house-trained.'

Dora's smile faded too at this remark. 'You no longer have a house to go to,' she reminded him softly.

Griffin gave another shrug. 'My mother will come around—eventually. And, in the meantime, I have your house to stay in.'

That was what she was afraid of. But he couldn't stay with her indefinitely. For one thing the neighbours would no doubt start speculating about the fact that a man had moved in with her only weeks after her father's death. And for another she simply didn't want Griffin that close to her. Even on a temporary basis!

'Besides,' Griffin continued dismissively, 'I haven't lived in a house for years. Even my apartment looks as if I've just moved in or I'm in the process of moving out!'

Dora knew exactly what he meant by that remark when they arrived at his apartment. There were packing boxes, either in the process of being unpacked or packed, standing in the sitting room.

It was an enormous flat for one person, with at least two bedrooms if not more, a kitchen and a bathroom leading off the main room. But all of them had that same half-lived-in-look. Perhaps with Griffin's constant travelling that was inevitable. Although Dora knew she couldn't have lived in this almost temporary way herself for any length of time...

'How long have you lived here?' she couldn't resist asking as she frowned across at Griffin.

He shrugged. 'I took the place on approval about a year ago, and brought all my stuff in.' He indicated the packing boxes. 'It's still only on approval!'

Which was rather sad, really, Dora thought. She had lived in the same house all her life, had put down roots there—and collected her unicorns! If she ever had to move it would take her weeks to pack everything up into boxes; Griffin looked as if he could do it in a couple of hours!

But he had said a year ago…about the time of Charles's death…

'I moved in here just after Charles died.' Griffin seemed to respond to her thoughts. 'Although at the time I thought— Well, never mind what I thought.' He grimaced. 'I'll only be a couple of minutes.' He hobbled towards one of the bedrooms. 'Make yourself at home,' he invited dryly.

As he, the occupant of the apartment for the last year, didn't seem to have done that, Dora didn't see how she could be expected to do so in a matter of minutes!

But she was drawn towards the over-full bookcase that ran the whole way along one wall—over-full because, once the shelves had become full, Griffin had started to pile the books on the carpeted floor in front of the bookcase.

Most of the books looked well read, including several of the titles Dora had acquired for him. She couldn't help wondering how, with his very busy lifestyle, Griffin ever found the time to read. But he obviously did. And enjoyed doing so.

At last Dora had found something the two of them had in common!

'Ready.' Griffin appeared in the bedroom doorway, having slung his overnight bag over one shoulder so that he could still continue to use both crutches.

Dora hurried over to take the bag from him, anxious now to be on her way. She didn't want to find anything the two of them had in common; it was easier, much easier, to keep telling herself the two of them were completely unsuited, and dismiss her feelings towards him in that way.

'Let's go, then,' she bit out, much more sharply than she

had intended, and received a narrow-eyed look from Griffin.

She chose to ignore him and turned away. She didn't want to know about Griffin's life, let alone get caught up with curiosity about it.

Which was the reason why, when they arrived at the television studio half an hour later, she refused to go inside with him!

She shook her head, not moving out from behind the wheel of the car. 'What time do you want me to come back for you?'

Griffin bent down to look in the car at her. 'Not star-struck, Izzy?' he drawled derisively.

'Not in the least,' she dismissed dryly. 'Just tell me what time to come back.'

'About five o'clock should do it,' he murmured thoughtfully. 'Are you sure you won't come inside? It's really quite interesting—'

'Griffin!' a female voice cried out concernedly. 'What on earth have you done? Oh, you poor darling!' The young, leggy brunette who had been making her way down the steps that led into the studio stopped by the car as she saw Griffin was on crutches. 'Can I help you inside?' She looked up at him with limpid blue eyes.

Griffin shot Dora a conspiratorial wink before turning to look at the other woman. 'How kind of you, Angela,' he murmured appreciatively. 'But weren't you just leaving?'

The woman gave him a dazzling smile. 'I'm more than happy to help you, Griffin,' she assured him throatily. 'Have you paid off the taxi?' She glanced uninterestingly at Dora as she sat behind the wheel.

Taxi? Dora inwardly echoed the word angrily. This woman thought she was a taxi driver? Not only was it a damned cheek, but it also implied that she simply didn't feel Dora was attractive enough to be anything else in Griffin's life. Wonderful!

'I'll come back for you about five o'clock, then—Mr Sinclair,' she bit out caustically, moving over to close the passenger door, almost shutting Griffin's fingers in it where he leant against the door for extra support.

Dora didn't even glance his way again before putting the car into gear and accelerating away, her face stonily averted as she did so.

The nerve. The cheek. The absolute damned cheek!

She gave herself an impatient glance in the driving mirror. Did she look like a taxi driver? What did taxi drivers look like...? All shapes, sizes and sexes, as far as she could remember. But even so! And Griffin had just stood there grinning at the mistake, damn him. No doubt enjoying himself. At her expense. Again.

She gave a rueful shake of her head, relaxing slightly. In the broadest sense of the word, she *was* Griffin's taxi this morning. As she would be again this evening.

But she had several things to organise before then, she realised briskly. The most important of those being to find someone to complete the work at the shop. At the current rate of progress, she might be able to re-open by Christmas!

By five-fifteen, sitting outside the studio waiting for Griffin to appear, Dora was slightly irritated.

By five-thirty she was very irritated.

By five-forty-five she had passed irritation and was well on her way to anger.

By six o'clock she was angry.

And by six-fifteen she was absolutely furious.

So much so that she stormed out of the car, up the steps, and burst into the reception area. Griffin hadn't even bothered to send a message out to her once he'd realised he was going to be delayed, let alone an apology! He—

'Can I help you?' the young receptionist enquiring brightly from behind her desk.

Dora drew in a deeply controlling breath, although her eyes still glittered deeply grey in her agitation. 'I'm here to collect Mr Sinclair, and—'

'Miss Baxter?' the other woman put in smoothly. 'He asked me to have you taken to the studio as soon as you arrived. If you would just take a seat for a moment, I'll—'

'Would you please inform Mr Sinclair that I shall be leaving in fifteen minutes? With or without him!' She spoke pleasantly enough; after all, it wasn't this woman's fault that Griffin was inconsiderate and selfish. 'If he's later than that, I suggest he call himself a taxi!' She turned on her heel and marched back outside to her car.

Her main reason for feeling so angry wasn't that Griffin might have been delayed, or even that he hadn't informed her; it was the fact she was inwardly sure he was doing this on purpose. He knew damned well she was supposed to be going out at seven-thirty this evening, and, even if he appeared in the next fifteen minutes, with the density of the traffic at this time of the evening she was going to be hard pushed to make it home by seven-thirty, let alone be ready to go out anywhere!

She had actually tried to contact Sam today, to cancel their date for this evening, but it was just her luck that it was his day off, and there had been no reply when she'd tried to telephone him at his apartment. She had finally called the hospital back and left a message there for him, cancelling their date tonight, just on the off-chance that he might check in there on a patient, or for some other reason during the day. But, as he hadn't telephoned her back, she didn't hold out much hope of his having received that message. And so, despite all her efforts, Sam was likely to turn up at the house for her this evening at seven-thirty.

And Griffin had four minutes left before she left him stranded here!

But, as she might have guessed, with barely two minutes to go of the allotted fifteen minutes, the glass doors at the front of the building swung open, and Griffin aided by a security man this time, made his way down the steps towards her car.

He grinned unabashedly at Dora as he reached the car, that beguiling, boyish smile—a smile that probably usually made most people forgive him most things. Today was his unlucky day!

Once again Dora made no effort to get out of the car, reaching over and thrusting the passenger door open for him. 'Get in,' she instructed through gritted teeth.

'Good evening to you too, Izzy,' he drawled mockingly as he bent down to thrust the crutches into the back of the car before levering himself inside.

Still Dora didn't move. She was too angry with him to feel the least sympathy for his obviously painful efforts. He had managed perfectly well all day—probably with the help of more gushing and beautiful women like the one this morning!—and as far as Dora was concerned he could damn well manage now!

She waited barely long enough for the car door to close behind him before accelerating away. It was almost a quarter to seven now. Griffin's struggle to get into the car had taken him almost another ten minutes, and there was no way, unless she broke every speed limit there was, that she was going to be home before Sam arrived at seven-thirty. And it was all Griffin's fault.

'Had a good day?'

Dora spared him only a brief, scathing glance. As it happened, she *had* had a good day, having miraculously found that the carpenter who had put in the railing could also spare her the time to finish the rest of the work. And probably before Monday too.

Consequently, when she'd driven to the studio to pick Griffin up, her mood had been happy and buoyant, but Griffin, with what she considered his deliberate tardiness, had wiped out those good feelings in one easy sweep!

She certainly wasn't in the mood to listen to the detailed account Griffin was now giving her of his own day. As if she cared! He had delayed her on purpose this evening because of her date with Sam, of that she was certain. He certainly hadn't been late on any of the other evenings when he had joined her at the shop! No, he had done this on purpose. Dora was sure of that.

'Is there something wrong?' Griffin prompted several minutes later, having received no response from her whatsoever to what had turned out to be his monologue.

Wrong!

He knew damn well what was wrong! And if he thought she was unaware of his deliberate plan to sabotage her date, he was mistaken.

'Izzy?' he prompted again softly. 'You aren't being very friendly this evening,' he complained.

Dora wondered if it were possible to actually have steam coming out of one's ears! It certainly felt like it to her at the moment, so heated was her anger.

'Friendly!' she repeated forcefully, her hands tightly gripping the steering wheel as she drove. 'Almost two hours I sat outside that damned studio waiting for you to appear—and you expect me to feel *friendly*?' she snapped furiously. 'You really are the most aggravating, annoying—'

'I love it when you say nice things to me,' he murmured with a satisfied smile.

A smile Dora would have dearly liked to wipe off his too-handsome features! '—selfish, uncaring—'

'Ah, now, I draw the line at uncaring,' he cut in with a frown. 'I wasn't late on purpose, you know, Izzy.'

'Weren't you?' she scorned disbelievingly. 'Somehow I find that very hard to believe, Griffin. You know damned well I'm supposed to be going out at seven-thirty.'

'You'll still make that,' he assured her stiffly. 'And it was as difficult working today, with this damned ankle and the crutches, as you predicted it would be. We had a meeting at the end of the day—the reason I'm late, incidentally—and decided to forget the rest of the week and try again on Monday, when hopefully I'll be a lot more mobile.'

Dora really wasn't interested in what they had decided! She was tired, agitated and hungry; not a very good combination at the best of times, let alone when Griffin was the one responsible for most of it!

'How nice.' She didn't even attempt to disguise her sarcasm.

Griffin chuckled softly at her side. 'Good to see you're getting your sense of humour back!' he mused dryly.

She gave him a sharp glance. 'I—' She broke off as she saw the laughter gleaming in his eyes. 'This isn't funny, Griffin.' She tried to sound stern, to hang on to the anger she had been feeling so strongly towards him.

But it was impossible with Griffin wearing that repentant little-boy look, the laughter gleaming in the deep green of his eyes.

'Okay, Griffin.' She relaxed back in her car seat, her shoulders aching from the tension she had been under until this moment. 'Let's call a truce,' she suggested wearily.

'Do we have to? You look beautiful when you're angry,' he drawled challengingly.

'Not again, Griffin!' Dora shook her head ruefully. 'It didn't work for you this morning—and it isn't going to work this time, either!'

'I know.' He gave a puzzled frowned. 'I can't understand what it is I'm doing wrong; that sort of line always works in the movies.'

The problem was that even when Griffin did it wrong a part of her was crying out, Yes, keep saying wonderful things like that to me! The part of her that was in love with him...

'People in films work to a script, Griffin,' she told him heavily. 'It's supposed to work. Because they aren't real people.' Reality, as she knew only too well, was that she and Griffin just weren't suited to each other, that they wanted different things from life, from a relationship.

Griffin just wanted fun and laughter from a relationship, with sex thrown in. She still wanted that fun and laughter—and there was no doubting that although Griffin could make her angrier than anyone else ever had, too—but she didn't just want sex, wonderful as she was sure that would be with Griffin. She wanted love and commitment, not to be someone Griffin left behind when he moved on to other things, other women.

'Pity,' he murmured, putting his head back against the seat, and he gave every impression of having fallen asleep.

Although that impression was quickly dispersed twenty-five minutes later, when they reached Dora's home.

With expected bad timing, after Griffin's unforgivable delay in leaving the studio, Sam's car was already parked outside the house. So he hadn't received her message...

Dora stopped the car behind Sam's, glancing towards the house to see Sam standing on the front doorstep, a puzzled frown on his face as he realised the house was empty. Even as Dora looked across at him he glanced at his watch, as if checking that he wasn't the one in error about the timing of his arrival.

But before Dora could even switch off the car engine, let alone open the car door, Griffin, for all his earlier struggle to get in the car, seemed to be having no trouble getting out of it now. In fact he was out on the pavement, crutches in his hands and making his way towards the house—and Sam!—before Dora had even made a move to get out.

'You must be Sam.' Dora heard him greet the other man as she scrambled out of the car just as Griffin reached Sam's side. 'Izzy—Dora—has told me all about you.'

Sam's already puzzled expression clearly showed that Dora hadn't so much as mentioned Griffin to him!

Which, of course, she hadn't! She hadn't even seen Griffin for almost a year when he'd turned up at the shop six weeks ago, and, although Sam had telephoned her a couple of times since her father died, she hadn't actually spent any time with him for over two months.

'Sorry we're a little late back,' Griffin told the other man lightly. 'Izzy has very kindly been acting as my chauffeur for the day.'

'She's a kind person,' Sam answered him warily, obviously still at a loss to know what was going on.

'Isn't she, though?' Griffin turned to give her an intimate smile. 'What man could possibly resist her?' he added possessively. 'I know I certainly couldn't. And luckily she reciprocates the feeling. Which is the reason we became engaged to each other yesterday evening,' he added with satisfaction.

Dora stared at him. Not only had he delayed her so that she couldn't possibly be ready to go out with Sam, but now he had told the other man about their bogus engagement.

What on earth did he think he was doing?

CHAPTER NINE

'GET out,' Dora bit out coldly, trembling with the deep anger burning within her.

'But—'

'I said get out, Griffin.' Her voice shook with anger now, her hands clenched tightly at her sides.

She had just experienced the most embarrassing five minutes of her life! She'd watched helplessly as Sam had verbally floundered at being told Dora was engaged to the other man, had inwardly cringed herself as he'd looked at her accusingly for not being the one to tell him. Her halting comment about leaving messages for him at the hospital had carried little weight in the forgiveness line as far as Sam was concerned.

Sam had given them his stilted congratulations, accompanied by a sickly grin, before taking his leave of them, walking back to his own car with stiff dignity. He'd even managed to give them an awkward wave before driving away, his features schooled into an expression of calm resolve.

Dora had known at that moment that, fiancé or not, she had seen the last of Sam, that he would never forgive her for the humiliation he had just suffered.

And it was all Griffin's fault. Arrogant, *uncaring* Griffin.

'He wasn't your type anyway, Izzy,' he announced now, with that same arrogance, as the two of them sat facing each other across the width of her kitchen like the adversaries they now were—in Dora's mind, at least. She no longer cared what Griffin thought—about Sam or anyone else.

And he had the nerve to accuse her father and Charles of trying to run her life for her; they were mere amateurs compared to this man!

'I have no intention of discussing anything to do with Sam with you,' she told Griffin icily. 'You've crossed over a line as far as I'm concerned. In fact, you've trampled all over it! And now I want you to leave.' Before she began to scream.

Because that was exactly what she felt like doing. Sam might not have been the most exciting man she had ever met, but he had been her choice of friend; how would Griffin like it if she strode into his life and started vetoing his friends? She knew the answer to that all too well!

'But—'

'No buts, Griffin,' she told him firmly. 'You humiliated Sam and you embarrassed me. And you did both of those things with a lie—a lie you used earlier to get your mother off your back.' Her expression hardened as she talked of the other woman. 'While I can understand the reason you felt the need to do that, it is nevertheless still a lie. And it certainly wasn't for repeating to any third parties,' she bit out caustically.

'How am I supposed to manage on my own?' Griffin chided ruefully. 'After all, I did sustain this injury while—'

'—helping me,' Dora completed with a weary sigh. 'That excuse has already worn thin, Griffin. You managed perfectly well on your own a short time ago when it came to getting out of the car and talking to Sam. In fact—' she grimaced '—you were quicker than me!' Otherwise this situation would never have arisen. She was sure she could have explained things to Sam, if she had been allowed to do so, in a way that would have saved any of them embarrassment. As it was… 'No, Griffin,' she told him firmly, 'that excuse isn't going to work with me any more. I just want you to go.'

'You—'

'To be quite honest, Griffin,' she added hardly, 'I found your behaviour this evening as domineering as you claim my father's and Charles's was,' she told him bluntly.

A nerve pulse in his cheek, but Dora couldn't be sure what was the cause of it—anger, or a direct hit with her blunt statement. Whichever, Griffin no longer looked mildly amused by her outrage. In fact, all the laughter had left his face and eyes. Perhaps she had finally got through to him…?

'I said those things for a reason, Izzy—'

'I know—you didn't like my father and you don't believe I ever loved Charles,' she scorned.

'You really liked him, didn't you?' Griffin rasped harshly.

Really liked who? Ah… 'Of course I liked Sam,' she answered, as she realised that was who he was talking about. 'I would hardly have gone out with him in the first place if I didn't like him.'

Griffin frowned darkly. 'I could always give him a call—'

'Please don't bother,' Dora dismissed coldly. 'I'm quite capable of doing my own explaining, thank you.' Although she knew that with Sam she never would; their friendship was over.

Her engagement to Griffin might be entirely fictional, but her love for him wasn't. What would be the point of explaining anything to Sam when that was the way things were—and were likely to remain!

'After you've left,' she added pointedly.

Griffin sighed. 'You won't even try to understand, will you?'

'What is there to understand, Griffin?' she challenged scornfully.

'The reason I behaved as I did with Sam, for one thing,' he said pointedly.

'Oh, I already know the reason you did that!' Mischief! Griffin was full of it. And he didn't seem to care who he hurt with it, either.

'I doubt it.' He shook his head. 'You don't have much of an opinion of me, do you, Izzy?'

That ridiculous name again.

Once Griffin had finally gone from her life, she would never hear it again...

She dampened down the pain in her chest at such a realisation. 'Have you ever given me any reason to think otherwise?'

She answered his question with one of her own. Because inside she was screaming. Of *course* she had an opinion of him; she loved him!

She loved that wicked sense of humour that often caused such mischief. She loved his kindness—the kindness that had allowed Charlotte to have her trouble-free wedding. She loved the way he looked—those same looks that millions of other women drooled over on the television when they watched his travel programmes.

Of course she had an opinion of him; but it was one she intended keeping to herself.

Always.

For to do anything else would be to open herself up to so much pain and humiliation. Besides, she was still furious with him.

'Never mind—it's taking far too long for you to think

of an answer!' he drawled self-derisively, shaking his head as he straightened. 'The problem with you, Izzy—'

'I don't think I'm the one with the problem,' she cut in dryly.

'—is that from the very first you wouldn't allow Dora to give me a chance,' he finished determinedly.

A chance to do what? Besides, Dora and Izzy were one and the same person. 'You—'

'Izzy looked at me, and she liked what she saw—oh, yes, you did, Izzy,' he insisted firmly, as she would have protested. 'Do you think I don't know when a woman finds me attractive? Give me credit for having some sensitivity,' he said dryly. 'Izzy Baxter liked me—'

'So did Fiona Madison,' she scorned, embarrassed colour in her cheeks. How could she have made herself, and her feelings, so obvious two years ago? It was humiliating!

Griffin gave her a reproving smile. 'That's the prudish Dora talking again now, so I'll forget you made that implication about Fiona and myself. She happens to be a family friend, and I had always promised her, and the husband she adored, that once Dungelly Court was up and running I would do a review of the place for her. If you don't believe me,' he drawled at Dora's sceptical expression, 'ask my mother; she happens to be Fiona's godmother!'

Dora had no intention of asking Margaret Sinclair anything; in fact, she never intended speaking to the other woman again. And she was sure Griffin was perfectly well aware of that. Besides, as far as she was aware, outrageous as Griffin could be, he had never lied to her...

She raised her chin challengingly. 'I really don't see what any of this has to do with me.'

'No, you wouldn't, would you—Dora?' he added pointedly. 'But when we were together at Dungelly Court—'

'We had dinner together,' she cut in heatedly. 'Don't make it sound more than it was!'

'Whatever.' He shrugged impatiently. 'That evening you allowed Izzy to talk for you—'

'There is no Izzy!' she burst out forcefully. 'How many times do I have to tell you that?' Her eyes blazed deeply grey.

He shook his head, giving a smile tinged with sadness. 'Oh, yes, there is an Izzy. Deny it all you like, Dora.' He humoured her as she would have protested again. 'But I'll never believe otherwise. Especially not after seeing your collection of unicorns this morning.' His eyes glowed at the memory. 'Izzy collected them, not Dora,' he insisted firmly.

She could feel the hot colour in her cheeks. No one, other than her parents, had ever seen her unicorns, or even knew that she collected them. Until Griffin...

'I will leave, Dora,' Griffin continued softly. 'But if you ever see Izzy, will you tell her I would love to see her again?'

She breathed shakily. 'Griffin—'

'I hope you'll be happy, Dora.' He clasped the tops of her arms, his gaze intent on the pallor of her face. 'Whatever, or whoever, is your choice for the future.'

'I— But where will you go?' Now that he was actually on the point of leaving she was filled with another sort of pain.

Because this time she knew he would never come back. There was only Dora here for him now, and he didn't particularly like her. Perhaps she was putting that a little too strongly, but Dora was too timid, too scared to take any risks in her life, to interest a man like Griffin.

'I'll manage.' He dryly quoted her own word back at her. 'One thing you can be sure of, though—I won't be

going anywhere near my mother!' he added. 'But to more
practical matters—how are you going to get the work done
at the shop?'

'I spoke to the carpenter today, and he says he can complete all the work for me,' she assured him dismissively.

Griffin smiled. 'No one is indispensable, hmm?' he murmured ironically, giving her arms a light squeeze before
releasing her. 'I'll send someone round for my car as soon
as it can be arranged.'

'There's no hurry,' she assured him huskily, bereft at the
loss of his touch.

'Oh, I think there is.' He nodded slowly. 'And I'm really
sorry if I messed things up for you with the doctor, Dora.'
He turned to pick up his crutches, missing the look of desperation that suddenly appeared on her face as she realised
he was leaving. 'Maybe the two of you were suited, after
all,' he added sadly.

There was no mockery in his tone this time, only sadness. Which made Dora feel like crying. In fact, she had
felt like crying for the last few minutes. Ever since Griffin
had accepted that he did have to leave.

And he was wrong; she and Sam weren't suited. Any
more than she and Charles had been—

What was she thinking? She had loved Charles, been
engaged to marry him, would have been married to him by
now but for the car accident that had taken him away from
her.

Wouldn't she...?

She looked up at Griffin with stricken eyes, tears blurring
her vision. She loved this man, in fact she realised she had
fallen in love with him two years ago. What would have
happened to her marriage to Charles when she had finally
realised that?

'Give the doctor a call, Dora,' Griffin advised harshly,

totally misunderstanding the reason for her tears. 'I'm sure he'll listen to what you have to say.'

Dora couldn't move as Griffin left the kitchen, and was still standing in the same spot when she heard the front door close a couple of minutes later. She had told Griffin to go. And he had.

Her tears now fell hotly against her cheeks. Griffin had gone. And she knew she would never see him again…

'Absolutely wonderful idea, my dear,' the woman told her gushingly as she left the bookshop. Dora locked the door behind her. It was five-thirty on a Saturday evening; time to go home. And that was something Dora delayed nowadays for as long as she possibly could. While she was at the shop she could keep herself busy—the changes she had made before the re-opening three weeks ago had been such a success that she'd taken on a full-time worker to help her out this last week. It was only when she was at home, in the otherwise empty house, that the futility of it all crowded in on her.

As she'd predicted, she hadn't seen Griffin again since the night she'd told him to leave. She'd told him she didn't want to see him again, and he had kept her to that. As promised, he had even had his car picked up from the back of the shop. Dora had found it gone when she'd gone into work one morning. Yes, Griffin had well and truly gone from her life.

And how she missed him!

Izzy, too.

Griffin was the only person who had ever realised there was an Izzy, and without him there to tease and cajole her, Izzy was slowly ceasing to exist at all…

'Dora!'

She turned from locking the shop door on her way out,

a smile of genuine pleasure lightening her features as she saw Charlotte hurrying along the pavement towards her. A Charlotte who, newly returned from her honeymoon, looked radiantly happy...

'I'm so glad I managed to catch you,' the other woman gasped breathlessly as she reached Dora's side. 'My goodness, Dora.' She grinned. 'I know I asked you to keep an eye on Griffin—but I had no idea you would actually become engaged to him!' She beamed her pleasure at the development.

Dora's smile faded as she stared at the other woman. 'Who told you that...?' she said warily.

She hadn't seen Griffin for the last three weeks, but she had assumed he would have informed his family by now that their engagement was a bogus one. Charlotte's greeting seemed to imply otherwise...

'My mother, of course.' Charlotte grimaced, instantly dispelling Dora's assumption that it was Griffin the other woman had been talking to. 'And Griffin too, of course, once my mother had told me the good news.'

Dora swallowed hard. 'I don't believe your mother thought of it in quite that way!' Exactly what had Griffin told his sister of their 'engagement'?

Charlotte gave a throaty chuckle. 'I'm not about to repeat what my mother said about it! And anyway, I didn't come here to talk about my mother,' she added briskly. 'Stuart and I are having our leaving dinner tomorrow evening at Stuart's apartment, and of course we want you and Griffin to be there.'

Dora was pleased to see the other woman, of course she was, but there was no way she could have dinner with Charlotte and her husband—and Griffin! 'I'm not sure—'

'Neither was Griffin. Which was why he told me to ask you.' Charlotte nodded. 'He explained that he's away tonight, but he'll be back in time for dinner tomorrow. He said that if it's okay with you it's okay with him. Oh, do say the two of you don't have any other plans,' she pleaded, clasping Dora's hands. 'Stuart and I go to New York on Monday, and it would be lovely if we could all spend tomorrow evening together before we go.'

Griffin had told Charlotte to ask her...?

What was she supposed to say to that? Why couldn't he have just told Charlotte the truth, that their engagement was purely a fiction of his own mind, a ploy to keep his mother's machinations at bay? As it was, he had left the decision for accepting or refusing the invitation to her—at the same time ensuring she couldn't even contact him to see what was going on!

She looked up undecidedly at Charlotte. She would be lying if she said she didn't want to see Griffin again. She had missed him these last three weeks, and even the obvious success of the shop hadn't helped fill the empty space he had left behind him. Besides, he obviously hadn't told Charlotte the truth, so why should *she*? And Griffin *had* left the decision about dinner with Charlotte and Stuart tomorrow evening to her...

'Okay, Charlotte,' she accepted firmly before she could have second thoughts. Those would come later! All she could think of at the moment was that she would see Griffin again tomorrow evening...

'Wonderful!' Charlotte beamed her pleasure. 'Stuart will come and pick you up.'

'There's no need for that.' Dora shook her head.

'Of course there is.' Charlotte gave her hands another squeeze before releasing them. 'Griffin is going to be late back, so he's coming straight to Stuart's apartment, and I don't think it's a good idea for you to drive into town; the champagne is going to be flowing pretty freely!'

And the way Dora felt at the moment, she might drink rather a lot of it!

'Are you sure Stuart won't mind?' She frowned her concern.

'He suggested it.' Charlotte smiled. 'It's probably his way of getting out of helping me with the last-minute arrangements! What he doesn't realise is I'll be glad of a few minutes' peace and quiet to do those things without anyone under my feet! Is seven o'clock okay for you?'

'Fine,' Dora accepted evenly. Her weekend wasn't exactly brimming over with things to do! In fact, she was going to have to make an effort to keep herself busy until tomorrow night—otherwise she might just 'chicken out', as Griffin had once put it, and not go at all!

'Lovely!' Charlotte looked very pleased with herself. 'I'll let you get off now; I'm sure you have lots to do!'

Not exactly. In fact, the silence of her home closed in on her as soon as she got in half an hour later and closed the door behind her.

Pull yourself together, Dora, she told herself firmly. She was going to see Griffin again tomorrow evening; that was a lot more than she had had an hour ago. Besides, she did have things to do here to keep her busy; she still had her father's things to sort out. And it was time she did it.

Charlotte had said Griffin was away. Who with? Was he seeing Amanda Adams again—?

Stop!

She had to stop thinking about Griffin. If she didn't she would go quietly insane.

Although finally making the decision to go through her father's bedroom, to sort through his clothes and papers, wasn't guaranteed to keep her sane, either!

But, after trying unsuccessfully on Saturday evening to keep thoughts of Griffin at bay, going through her father's room was exactly what she decided to do on Sunday morning. In a few more hours she would see Griffin again, and she had to keep herself busy until then.

Besides, it was time.

Past time.

Two hours later Dora sat on the floor of her father's bedroom, one of the drawers from his dressing table on the floor in front of her, a totally dazed look on her face. For at the back of this particular drawer had been a large brown envelope marked 'Private', and after several minutes of wondering if she should look inside she had finally decided she would have to. There was no one else to do it, after all...

There had been two envelopes inside, and at first Dora had thought they might be letters from her mother to her father. There had been few separations between the married couple, but that didn't mean they had never written to each other. In which case Dora would have been loath to read them. Her father had been an emotionally distant man, her mother had been youthfully exuberant, but somehow their marriage had worked, and the two of them had been very much in love. Dora didn't want to intrude on that relationship by reading their letters to each other.

But the postmarks on both letters assured her they couldn't possibly have been from her mother; both of them were dated several years after her death.

It was the biggest shock of Dora's life to discover, on opening them and simply looking at the signature on the bottom of both, that that signature was 'Griffin Sinclair'!

She again looked at the postmarks on both letters; the first one was dated only two months after she and Griffin had met at Dungelly Court, the second was dated six months later.

She had never known anything about Griffin writing to her father once, let alone twice!

What did it mean?

The only way she would discover the answer to that was to read the two letters. And, with trembling hands, that was exactly what she did...

CHAPTER TEN

'HELLO, Griffin,' Dora greeted him huskily.

Stuart had hurried off to the kitchen to see Charlotte after showing Dora into the sitting room where Griffin stood. Alone.

She felt so nervous. She wanted to see him, *needed* to see him, but she would rather it weren't under these circumstances. She needed to talk to him privately, and there was no way she could do that when they were here to have dinner with his sister and her husband!

Griffin looked wary, obviously unsure of her reaction at being railroaded into coming here for dinner, as his fiancée, when the two of them hadn't so much as spoken for three weeks!

But that wasn't all he looked. If Dora had found the last three weeks a strain to get through—her short black dress slightly looser now than it should be—then Griffin didn't look as if he had fared much better. His face was thinner, gaunt almost, and he no longer looked healthy and tanned. His dinner suit seemed to hang on him; the shirt looked slightly too big around the collar.

His eyes had no spark of humour in them, either, as if he found very little to laugh about nowadays. In fact, tonight Griffin looked every one of his thirty-four years!

'Dora,' he greeted distantly, not a hint of a limp in his movements, no crutches in sight, either.

'Your ankle is better, I see?' she observed brightly, trying not to show the pain she felt at his use of the name Dora.

'Yes—thank you,' Griffin replied stiltedly, eyeing her warily, neither of them making any move to sit down. 'So if you're worried about the possibility of my suing you for damages—'

'I'm not in the least worried about that, Griffin,' she protested.

There was so much she needed to say to him! She still found it difficult to take in the significance of those letters he'd written to her father.

And could she really blame Griffin for feeling the way he obviously did? First her father, and then Dora herself. Both of them had told Griffin, at some stage, to get out of her life. She'd been stunned, then elated by what was written in the letters she had brought with her in her handbag. But both those letters had been written some time ago; maybe Griffin no longer meant what he had said...

She looked at him searchingly now, trying to read his emotions in the harsh severity of his face, in the cold, unfathomable depths of his eyes. There was nothing there but bleak bitterness, the latter an emotion she had never seen in Griffin before today.

'Griffin—'

'Here we are,' Charlotte announced, as she came in with a tray of hot canapés, effectively putting an end to what Dora had wanted to say to Griffin. 'Stuart is just bringing in the champagne. To toast your engagement!' she told Dora and Griffin excitedly. 'I can't tell you how thrilled I am that the two of you have got together at last!'

Dora gave Griffin a look from beneath lowered lashes; they hardly looked like an ecstatic newly engaged couple!

But Charlotte, still enchanted by her own happiness, seemed unaware of any friction. 'To both of you!' she toasted when they all had a glass of champagne. 'I had thought of inviting Mother here tonight,' she said derisively once they had all dutifully sipped their champagne. 'But I didn't see why she should ruin all our fun!' she added mischievously.

Dora felt a shiver down her spine just at the mention of Margaret Sinclair. Griffin had been right—her father and his mother had been so alike; neither of them had been content to let their children find love in their own way, both had had other ambitions and plans for them...!

The evening was an ordeal for Dora to get through. Griffin barely spoke, in fact he hardly looked at her, either, and her hopes that they might be able to talk things out— hopes that Griffin's letters had given her—faded rapidly as the evening progressed. Although Griffin had been instrumental in including her in this evening, he now seemed to be bitterly regretting it.

'Let us know as soon as you decide when the wedding is to be,' Stuart told them both warmly when it came time to leave. 'Charlotte and I will obviously fly home.'

'We wouldn't miss it for the world,' Charlotte added excitedly, her arm linked through her husband's as they walked Dora and Griffin to the door.

Wedding...! The chances of her and Griffin marrying each other were virtually nil. Dora groaned inwardly, barely aware of returning the newly married couple's hugs goodbye before preceding Griffin out through the door.

The two of them went down in the lift in complete silence.

Charlotte and Stuart had assumed Dora would be going home with Griffin, and after the miserable evening Dora had just spent she hadn't had the heart to say otherwise. No doubt she would be able to find a taxi once she was outside; it was a sure fact Griffin wouldn't want to drive her home!

But first she had to at least try to talk to Griffin, to let him know she'd never known of his visit to her father, or the letters he had sent him...

Standing downstairs in the foyer, she couldn't even look at him. This new Griffin seemed totally unapproachable. Something she had never, ever found him before...

'I'm sorry about all that up there.' He was finally the one to speak. 'Charlotte telephoned me yesterday just as I was leaving on a business trip, and I really didn't have the time to go into details with her.' He shook his head. 'I'm surprised you didn't tell her the truth and save yourself the bother of having to go through any more time pretending to be my fiancée.' he added harshly.

'I needed to see you, Griffin.' She took a deep breath. 'I found these in my father's bedroom; I believe they belong to you.' She was searching through her handbag, finally finding and holding out the two letters towards Griffin.

He glanced down at them, obviously recognising them by the way his mouth tightened, but he made no effort to take them from her. 'I don't think so,' he dismissed gruffly. 'Letters belong to the person they are addressed to, not the person who wrote them.' He continued to ignore the two letters she held out to him, hands thrust deep into his trouser pockets now.

Her own hand dropped back down to her side. 'Griffin...' She moistened her lips. 'I had no idea— My father didn't tell me—' She swallowed hard. 'I never knew you tried to find me again after we left Dungelly Court.'

Griffin's first letter to her father told her that he had. It also said that he was in love with her...

She hadn't been able to believe it this morning when she'd read those two letters. Griffin had been in love with her two years ago. He had come in search of her so that he could tell her of that love. And instead he had met her father. And been lied to… No wonder he had disliked her father so much!

Griffin shrugged, sighing heavily. 'It doesn't matter now, surely,' he dismissed warily.

Of course it mattered! One of the things that had always troubled her was the fact that he had never tried to find her again after they'd left Dungelly Court.

'It does matter, Griffin,' she protested heatedly. 'My father—' She swallowed again. 'My father told you I was engaged to someone else when you came to the house in search of me!'

The first letter to her father from Griffin had thanked him for his time, and for letting him know of Dora's engagement. Griffin had also asked that if ever that situation changed for her father to please let him know…

Griffin shrugged again. 'I half expected it; you had told me yourself that you had someone else in your life.'

'I was talking about my father!' she explained emotionally. 'I— You frightened me at Dungelly Court. I had never met anyone like you before—'

'Or I you,' he put in.

She felt the heat in her cheeks. 'You were right about me. I did allow myself to be Izzy there, to—to be attracted to you,' she added awkwardly.

Griffin's mouth twisted humourlessly. 'You frightened poor Dora out of her wits!'

'Oh, *damn* Dora,' she dismissed impatiently. 'Griffin I *wasn't* engaged to anyone else—'

'Six months later you were,' he reminded her grimly. 'You were engaged to my own brother! How your father must have enjoyed the irony of that. When I challenged him on the lie he had told me six months earlier, he told me that I wasn't good enough for you, that I didn't even have a proper job, let alone somewhere to live. He wanted something better for his only daughter, his only child, than a homeless travel writer. He saw that ''something better'' in my politician brother Charles!' he added grimly. 'A man obviously going places!'

She'd been able to tell all that by the tone of the second letter Griffin had written to her father. Griffin had obviously been furious at the lies he had previously been told. But Griffin had also assured her father that, although he believed that her father's motives for lying to him six months ago were questionable, to say the least, he accepted Dora's engagement to Charles, and would never try to interfere in that relationship.

Her father should have known from that letter what sort of man Griffin was; an honourable and honest one. Much more so than her father had ever been!

But her father had deliberately kept Griffin and herself apart two years ago, and if she'd never found those two letters he might have continued to do so. If she couldn't get through to Griffin now, if he didn't still feel the same way about her, then her father might still win...!

She had always thought, despite his reserve, that her father had loved her. And perhaps he had. But it had been a possessive, destructive love, a love that hadn't allowed her the freedom to love where she chose. Because two years ago she'd fallen for Griffin, and had just buried that love away when she thought he had just looked on their meeting as a game.

She looked at Griffin now, her eyes swimming with unshed tears. 'It's too late, isn't it?' she realised heavily; Griffin looked so hard and unapproachable, so unlike the man she'd thought she knew. So unlike the man she loved...

Griffin sighed impatiently. 'Too late for what, Dora?'

His deliberate use again of that name for her cut into her

like a knife. As she was sure it was supposed to. All the time he had loved her, and she had done nothing but push him away.

'What your father did to us was wrong.' He nodded tersely. 'But perhaps he did us both a favour. How many times have you told me yourself how unsuited we are?' he added wryly.

Dora and Griffin, perhaps. But not *Izzy* and Griffin!

She was hurt and stunned by her father's betrayal, but she was even more stunned by the fact that Griffin had loved her. Now her father was dead, and so unchallengeable, but she and Griffin were still very much alive. And she refused to leave until she heard it from Griffin's own lips that he no longer loved her!

'My unicorn collection is in a glass case in the sitting room now, Griffin,' she told him evenly, hoping he would realise what she was trying to tell him. Finding Griffin's two letters had freed Izzy, and she never intended to disappear behind the cautious Dora again.

He swallowed hard, a nerve pulsing in his rigidly held jaw. 'That's nice for you,' he finally murmured noncommittally.

Her eyes were so flooded with tears now she could hardly see him. 'Help me, Griffin!' she pleaded shakily.

He drew in a ragged breath. 'I don't know what you want me to do! Do you want me to talk to Sam for you after all? Is that it—?'

'Oh, damn Sam!' she burst out emotionally. 'Damn my father too. And damn Charles!' The three men were all the same. They had all wanted something from her, something that didn't include her own happiness or allow her to be herself.

Griffin had never done that. In fact, he had insisted he

wouldn't have anything to do with Dora, was prepared only
to see Izzy again!

'Haven't you realised yet, Griffin, that if I had known
you tried to find me two years ago, that my father sent you
away, I would never have become involved with Charles?
Or Sam? That I would have defied my father, would have
defied anyone, just so that I could be with you?' She stood
mere inches away from him now. 'Griffin, I love you. I've
always loved you. I just never believed—until today—that
you could ever love someone like me,' she groaned.

'Izzy...?' He looked uncertain now, totally unlike the
forceful Griffin she had always known.

'Yes—Izzy! Oh, Griffin.' She put her hands imploringly
on his arms. 'Please believe me when I say I've always
loved you! Even when I've been so angry with you I could
have—'

'Kissed me?' Griffin murmured, before his mouth came
down on hers in a kiss like no other they had ever shared.

Griffin still loved her! It was there in the searching gen-
tleness of his kiss, in the raw emotion he no longer had to
hide from her because he'd believed his feelings weren't
reciprocated.

'Marry me, Izzy?' He held her at arm's length, looking
down at her anxiously, obviously still not quite sure how
this had all come about.

She reached up and cradled either side of his beloved
face with hands that trembled slightly. 'I would have married you years ago if you'd asked me. Would have gone
against my father, your mother—anyone who tried to stop
us. Do you believe me?' She looked up at him with clear
grey eyes.

He looked down at her searchingly for several long seconds, and then he crushed her back into his arms. 'I believe

you! What a hell of a lot of time the two of us have wasted, Isadora Baxter—soon-to-be-Sinclair!'

Dora snuggled comfortably in his arms, smiling wickedly as she rested her head against his chest. 'Your mother is going to hate that!'

'What was it you said earlier? Damn my mother! Actually...' Griffin chuckled wryly '...I don't think my mother cares one way or another who I marry any more! I told her a couple of weeks ago, in no uncertain terms, that I would never enter the political arena,' he explained at her questioning look. 'That I would never marry Amanda Adams, either—'

'You seemed to like her well enough at Charlotte's wedding,' Dora remembered jealously.

Griffin shook his head ruefully. 'Only because I could see you didn't like her one little bit!'

'Well, of course I didn't,' she admitted impatiently. 'I can't stand seeing you with other women.'

'Well, you never will again,' he assured her huskily.

She believed him, knew beyond doubt now that Griffin loved her. 'You were telling me about your mother?' she reminded him softly.

'So I was,' he murmured with amusement, once again the relaxed Griffin Dora knew so well. 'With such disappointing children, my mother has decided to take matters into her own hands—she's going to marry Jeffrey Adams and become a political wife herself once again!'

Dora looked up at him in disbelief. Margaret had been a widow for years...! But she could see that Griffin, for all he was teasing about it, was completely serious about the forthcoming marriage. And why not? It was the obvious answer, really. It was a pity Margaret hadn't thought of it earlier!

'How amazing!' Dora finally breathed dazedly.

'How convenient,' Griffin corrected with satisfaction. 'She isn't going to have the time in future to be a nuisance to us,' he said happily.

Dora joined in his satisfied laughter. Jeffrey Adams could have no idea what he was taking on in having Margaret for his wife. Or perhaps he did... Margaret had apparently been a good political wife to Simon Sinclair, and Jeffrey Adams was definitely an ambitious politician. One thing Jeffrey need never worry about, and that was having his wife's support. He would probably be Prime Minister before he knew where he was!

'Griffin,' Dora murmured softly, unable to look at him as she played with one of the buttons on his shirt. 'After Charles—when he died—why didn't you—?'

'Come and declare my love for you, in spite of your father?' He grimaced.

'Yes.' She met his gaze steadily, searchingly.

'I thought perhaps you might really have loved him.'

'You've been telling me for weeks now that I didn't!'

'Wishful thinking, I'm afraid,' Griffin admitted ruefully. 'It's all right if you did, Izzy—'

'No—it isn't.' She gave a firm shake of her head. 'And neither is my giving you the impression there has ever been a man on—intimate terms in my life.' Embarrassed colour darkened her cheeks. 'There never has been, Griffin. Not Charles. Not any man.'

His arms tightened about her possessively. 'There is now,' he assured her huskily.

'I have to tell you about Charles first—explain what happened,' she insisted softly. 'Then we need never talk about it again. I—I was flattered by Charles's attention at first. Actually, I was still a little raw from my encounter with you at Dungelly Court,' she admitted, acknowledging his teasing smile with a rueful one of her own. 'Charles was handsome, obviously successful in his career, and he picked me as the person he wanted to share that with.' She shook her head. 'But the whole thing became a nightmare the day I found out the two of you were brothers! I'd heard so much about Charles's disreputable younger brother—the women—'

'Do you remember a few weeks ago you said that if we ever exchanged confidences on past relationships mine would take all night to tell you about?' He looked down at her intently as she slowly nodded. 'There hasn't been any woman since I met you at Dungelly Court. It's true, Izzy. If I couldn't have you, I certainly didn't want any pale substitutes.'

'But you always had—someone with you when you came back to the house at weekends,' she recalled painfully.

'A different someone every time.' He nodded. 'Camouflage, I'm afraid, Izzy. If you were going to marry my big brother, I certainly wasn't going to let you see just how much it was hurting me!'

'That makes this last year, since Charles died, even less understandable.' She frowned up at him.

'It was ten months and two days until I saw you again,' Griffin corrected wryly. 'But who was counting?'

Obviously he had been! 'Griffin, you weren't doing the "gentlemanly" thing, were you?' She remembered he had once said this was his mother's single claim to success in his upbringing.

His mouth twisted. 'I wanted you to be completely free of all past relationships before I came back into your life. Besides,' he added ruefully, 'your father's motives may have been wrong, but after thinking about it a while I decided that what he had said wasn't, I *didn't* have a permanent home, or a job that I took as seriously as I should have done. I decided that it was partly up to me to show that I was capable of being the sort of son-in-law, the sort of husband, your father wanted for you. Which is why I took on the apartment and signed a television contract. How could I possibly have guessed you would become involved with someone else before I came back into your life a changed man?' He looked down at her reprovingly.

He wasn't a 'changed man' at all! And, given the chance to choose for herself, she would have married Griffin two years ago—permanent home, responsible job or not!

'We've already discussed Sam,' she dismissed with a smile. 'He was the same camouflage for me that those women were for you.' She was pleased beyond belief that there had been no one else for Griffin since they'd met two years ago. She was also aware that it made her two relationships seem positively promiscuous in comparison. 'Where shall we live once we're married?' She changed the subject, putting the past exactly where it belonged—behind them. 'There's no way we can live in my father's house.'

'Actually, technically it's your house now, but I agree with you.' Griffin grimaced his distaste for the idea. 'And the apartment isn't exactly right either. Let's buy somewhere completely new—somewhere big enough for our children. Lots of children,' he added gruffly. 'All of them as beautiful as their mother.'

Griffin wanted their children too!

'Do you remember you once asked me about my mother?' she said slowly. 'What she was like?' She gave a little smile as he nodded. 'Well, she was outgoing, vivacious, loved to tease, loved life.'

'Like me?' Griffin realised what she was trying to say.

She hadn't fallen in love with a man in the mould of her father, which Charles had been, and Sam too, but with a male version of her effervescent mother...

'I love you, Griffin Sinclair,' she told him huskily, knowing he was that 'right man' for her they had once discussed.

'And I love you, Izzy Baxter,' he assured her gruffly. 'With all my heart. And for always.'

Yes, he loved her. She didn't doubt it now, and she knew she never would.

Izzy was here to stay…!

Yes, she would always be Izzy from now on, and was no longer afraid of loving or being loved. Not if it was Griffin she was in love with and Griffin who loved her in return.

'How about we get out of here,' Griffin murmured throatily, looking around at their public surroundings, 'and I show you just how much I love you?'

'Yes, please,' she accepted shyly.

He chuckled huskily. 'And tomorrow, my darling—tomorrow I'm taking you out and putting my engagement ring on this finger.' He kissed the third finger of her left hand. 'To be quickly followed by a wedding ring!'

It couldn't happen soon enough for Dora. They had already wasted enough time!

'Yes, please to that too!' she told him happily, her hand in his as the two of them went out into the night.

Together.

Always.

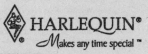

HARLEQUIN ◆ PRESENTS®

Passion™

Looking for stories that **sizzle**?

Harlequin Presents® is
thrilled to bring you romances
that turn up the **heat!**

Every other month there'll be a
PRESENTS PASSION™ book by
one of your favorite authors.

Next month look out for
AUNT LUCY'S LOVER
by **Miranda Lee**
On sale April 2000,
Harlequin Presents® #2099

Pick up a **PRESENTS PASSION**™—
where **seduction** is guaranteed!

Available wherever Harlequin books are sold.

◆ HARLEQUIN®
Makes any time special ™